MOON CURSOR

ROCCO SCIBETTA

ISBN 978-1-955156-81-3 (paperback)
ISBN 978-1-955156-82-0 (digital)

Rushmore Press LLC
1 800 460 9188
www.rushmorepress.com

Printed in the United States of America

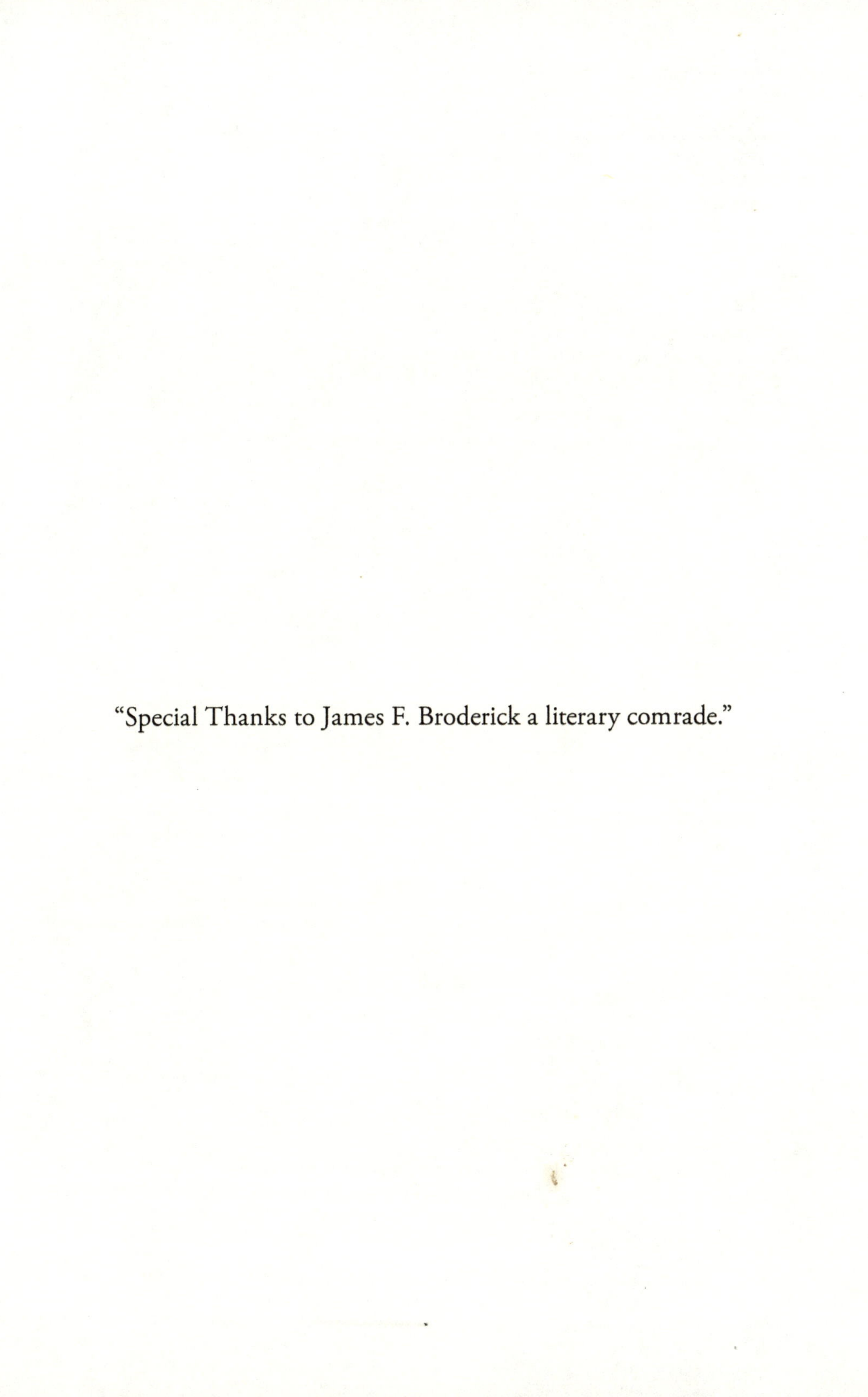

"Special Thanks to James F. Broderick a literary comrade."

"The sea refreshes our imagination because it does not make us think of human life; yet it rejoices the soul, because, like the soul, it is an infinite and impotent striving, a strength that is ceaselessly broken by falls, an eternal and exquisite lament. The sea thus enchants us like music, which, unlike language, never bears the traces of things, never tells us anything about human beings, but imitates the stirrings of the soul. Sweeping up with the waves of those movements, plunging back with them, the heart thus forgets its failures and finds solace in an intimate harmony between its sadness and the sea's sadness, which merges the sea's destiny with the destinies of all things."

— Marcel Proust, The Complete Short Stories of Marcel Proust

DUNES PSYCHIATRIC FACILITY HOSPITAL ROOM

I study the insects here in my room. I watch them change shapes. I once observed a cocoon give birth to a family of praying mantis outside my window. This is only natural and right according to God's law; however, maenads are not like that.

My room is a crayon box of van Gogh yellows checkered greens and blues. It is not quite a cell, but the windows are barred. The walls are a palimpsest. The markings of the truly insane that have slept here bleed through the walls, deeply carved markings of desperation show through the heavy paint in the same way my real personality sometimes comes through this overly medicated persona they insist I live in daily.

Someone scratched their nails into the wall blistering the plaster; another drew a skull in pen, the more romantic left bits and pieces of senseless poetry unable to be read in its entirety. My favorite is a drawing someone did on a smear of wall plaster, This visually articulate human being abstracted the image of four Barbie dolls eating hot dogs and drinking soda next to our Lady of Fatima while the baby Jesus is playing Tc tac toe. You could study the lunatic art on these walls forever, The best is the ghost images that bleed through the cheap paint over; mostly pale blues, they always use a light blue or tinted gray; ink and magic marker bleed the best.

I am not mad. And Aggie was not mad. I know she suffered from Hyperthymesia; a rare abnormality that leads people that have it to recall large amounts of life experiences in vivid detail. She was not able to forget. Nor could she block things out as we did so artfully at the Atlas Yacht club.

No, Aggie Fitz Oswald was not mad in the textbook sense; she was crippled by the horror; as well as the memory of incestualized abuse. However, with that being said, her gift for memory went far beyond that of her given life years. Her Maenad bloodline most certainly has something to do with that, although no doctor here would understand it. It is not in medical books or journals; you would have to probe deeply into the occult as The Magister Ludi has done. I was no believer; in fact, I was the greatest skeptic.

I was not there when her nervous system collapsed for the last time. Nor was I permitted to see her when old Fitzy had locked her away in the bell tower. Only that one time from the window when Fitzy died; her skin ashen and her eyelids burnt from the sun. The body was taken out to sea, not even a decent burial. The town was silent, the town was always silent.

A study in gray is her story in a way…all the way.

My name is Conliffe, Charlie Conliffe; I am on my way to a place of my youth, Key Harbor. The train will bring me as far as Throckmorten interchange from there I will taxi a ride to Constable Hook, it's an old part of town, quaint for the most part, sealed off and decrepit for the lower half. a little arm projects out from an old unchartered section long forgotten. It is a broken down passage to the Old Spye section. Once rich in history the old spye section was an original port for colonial traders and all types of related business.

It was documented in the town archives as being an entrance port to many foreign ships as well as English soldiers and Spanish manes. The coastal tranquility and sweeping harbor side romantic vista bounded along horseshoe bay and tipped out to just under the port of entry. A separating space of about ten miles leads the eye to a stretch of rocks that completes the horseshoe shape, later referred to as the key, thus becoming the vital access for Dutch trade and commerce close to three centuries ago.

"From whence there were trade and commerce in those days, "days of yore" as it was once quoted in school books and wives tales, it was not long before some Pirates ships would make entry to unload their bounty, stock food and drink philandering local wanton women folk. Legend had it that some treasures were laid in-store and hidden throughout the colorful old spye section; however, nothing as quixotic as a buried treasure was ever recovered. Over the years the town underwent a renovation, urban upheaval, and change; only minor trinkets and artifacts were unearthed, that was all.

A sword and wooden chest were discovered believed to belong to Captain Blood Raleigh in a bin of bum treasure junk belonging to a squatter by name of Amstel Tulles at the beginning of the 19tn century right here in the wrecks of the old mine called Sybil's cave, that was where Amstel Tulles squatted at the time; Sybil's cave was a natural water spring attached to the last remaining mansion of a rich industrialists playground from back in the 1700s. The undeveloped waterfront of this place attracted people of some means and millionaire types to visit constable hook in those days for its quiet seclusion and seaside amenities.

The affluent of those days would come from as far as Chicago and New Amsterdam to mingle and rub elbows with other board industrialists sharing prominent names as the Cartwright's and Wilmington's. Here their sons and daughters would marry to carry on the family crest until winds of time and change gusted forth grinding even the hardest family tradition and diamond ring into sand and wire.

The colony trade also brought with its cargo of a more visceral type. Prison ships or Hulks would sometimes come into port with prisoners from as far as New South Wales to use as a type of slave labor for some of the more prominent land developers who needed the strong backs of men in a tradeoff for freedom in a new world. Most were not hardened criminals or insane but young men who were destined to get off to a bad start due to environmental disadvantages; Ignorant near do wells that for all intents and purposes would most likely find themselves dangling from the end of a rope if not for the opportunity to sail off and work in the colonies clearing woods and breaking stones for little or no pay accept for food and housing.

They were mostly Dutch, skimmed from English principalities shipped off and forgotten about to make something of themselves or die trying. A section of the undeveloped and undesirable forest region of land was designated to them as a work camp. They were left to themselves to pilot the land. Offshore a bit and deeper into the woods is a scattered section of makeshift cottages and a self-contained village managed and sequestered by the offspring of the original Cropsey whites. These were once picturesque seaside bungalows back in the day. My friends and I, Sean Anthony and John Morris were brought here by our parents for vacation every summer for fun and relaxation throughout our teenage years. Except for the financial interests my folks had in historical property here, my aforementioned friends arrived serendipitously following the whims of their parents to seaside bungalows and fishing boats merely as appendages to their elders and betters.

One day we all met up innocently playing in the sand and later during our high school years formed the Atlas Yacht club, My room has become a kind of wunder Krammer; not quite as fascinating as Captain Fitzy's, "The old sea salt" Oh, I never told you about the wunder Krammer.

They have a history here, a tedious tainted tradition- to those who stay here long enough...of whitewashing their fences... Ha, ha,- that is, you know; making things go away. There is a cute nomenclature for the folks that have lived here all their lives, they are known as Harbor rats a lovely bunch of backstabbing weasels immoral in every way.

It was here that the Cropsey section was established around the time of the first settlers. Constable Leopold Cropsey was the purveyor of the land and the section became known as the Cropsey Hills. The inhabitants of that place became stereotyped as the Cropsey whites.

Off the wharf, about one half of a mile stood the shanty remnants of the old spye inn. It was condemned for the most part except that my family owned the property by some fathered in contract my Grandfather had with the town from over a century ago. When the property came to me I could have had it knocked down and rebuilt into a modern hotel, It was scenic and picturesque for Key Harbor which was enjoying the windfall from a renaissance that was taking over the whole waterfront from the Cape Anne annex to Keyport spring.

There is a tale I need to tell; a happening that needs to be told, although no one speaks of it here. They only talk of gibberish; speak of common things, simple threads of speech that form woven shrouds of folklore; the talk that binds small-town folks together.

The folks around here think I am crazy for not selling out, one of the many reasons they have come to question my sanity. However, I have my reasons. It is in a historical section and I would like to keep it that way. The Olde spye inn has been a tavern to these parts as recent as the late 1800s; it has been supplying food and quarter to the old salts and mercantile traders since the town's first renaissance just after the revolution. But, that is not the entire reason. There is a secret I hold with some friends, a childhood ritual you might say, that neither I nor my Comrades can outgrow or relinquish. For near twenty years the relic of that broken down colonial tavern has been home to our own Atlas yacht club.

It began as a game the Atlas Yacht club did, a romantic get together to tell stories on stormy nights and light candles; sometimes a flashlight was brought in but quickly discouraged by the core of the group that being (the magister Ludi) who insisted that everything remain as dark academia: John Morris, Sean Anthony and Myself, Charlie Conliffe. The group never quite grew beyond us three. Most of the other kids and future inductees moved on; they got bored with it, or just did not share our creepy curiosity for stale poetry and the morbid things we three had in common.

There are many talks and popular commentary these days of hauntings. It has become novel to narrators and scriptwriters to wax on about ghosts that inhabit houses and cellars; demons that possess the body and mind; some writers might do well to add artistic license and hyperbole to the simple shadows and glooms brought on by the performance of light and dark that each of us encounters as children. But this I can assure you is not fantasy. There is blood in the water of this putrid harbor; even after I burned most of it to the ground. The blood congeals like a tar pit beneath the earth.

It is here in this barbaric gulag for the criminally insane that I continue to write as part of my therapy, the twisting journal of rants and hallucinations of a sequestered mad man.

No one believes me and I have no friends here, only professional sycophants and academic assholes that by the power invested in them by the rite of a framed page of sheepskin that graces their office wall do they have the power to pass judgment over me. This lone document of university permits them right of entry into the business of occult and supernatural affairs that I have locked into the memory of my experiences.

Oh, I am not really on my way to Key Harbor. You see, that is a little joke I concocted for when Dr. Bursar probes into my past. Whatever I conjure up in memory I relive in fantasy. I have spent the last five years of my life here drugged and sequestered at the Dunes, a municipal mental hospital for the criminally insane, (The Dunes), a chocolate-box name to avoid stigmas for the local folks that live nearby.

"Dunes for Loon's" is how they casually refer to us and that is okay with me. They have the little hell that keeps them up at night, their dirty little seaside secrets, and the horror right off the coast in those caverns; a virtual rat's nest for any well-adjusted out of town sucker that casually gets entwined with this rabble.

The bars and taverns are quaint old buckets of blood that seem picturesque from a passing car window. Little American flags and over-grown gardens adorn picket fence communities in need of a new coat of paint implying patriotic elderly life therein; colonial-style spiny chairs rock to and fro on empty porches. The old statuary and Victorian shambles are gone.

A new wave of young "upwardly mobile" types began to encroach on our shores, but soon found the place not quite genteel enough for their liking and moved on. The demon force that controls this shanty bit of real-estate wedged neatly between two tourist havens at the Jersey shore embodies in personality the Thomas Hudson character made popular by Hemingway in his novel Islands in the stream. They wanted things to stay just as they were, they could be cruel to strangers, but yet my friends and I stumbled in and was accepted.

THE ATLAS YACHT CLUB

"If Bacchus ever had a color he could claim for his own, it should surely be the shade of tannin on drunken lips, on John Keats purple-stained mouth; or perhaps, of Homers dangerously wine-dark sea."

Victoria Finlay-

They were comic books, then dime-store novels greasy kid pulp that creates your first round of identity. Somebody tells you a folktale, somebody else knows someone who saw a ghost or heard a noise. You one day get to a place like this; an open book right on the water. An abandoned bell tower in your back yard, a haunted boat you want to explore. Your literary dreams branch out as you're your teenage hormones kick in.

Someone smuggles in a true confessions magazine or some underground nudie books; you can't be open about this kind of thing so you find a secret place to call your clubhouse. You get older go to colleges and universities, the sense of arcadia darkens, festering with tales from Washington Irving and Edgar Allen Poe. Sometimes you wish you could have met Mary Shelley, or had some brandy with Bram stoker because there would be so much to talk about. Some people walk around boardwalks with parrots, some have grimalkin cats in their New York apartments that paw at candle flames on rainy nights.

I met someone who recited Shakespeare; an old thespian. It was New York City Washington square… not far from the university. He collected welfare and lived with an old whore who was banging independently wealthy college students supporting themselves on family trust funds. After a while, you go through the phonies and the weekend warriors and realize there are no real pirates here. The folk songs and the smoky night spots collect dust and the dust collectors flock to them.

However, after a while, it is time to move on and I aligned myself with the few soulmates that have banded together from the beginning. We could never do anything else we three; Sean Anthony, the Magister Ludi, and me. Since we were kids meeting by the dilapidated Old Spye inn we told stories, read poetry, and romanticized about being bigger than ourselves, bigger than the sea; because we could not do anything else. We were not cool, we were not particularly brainy and not any of us were going to go on to perform anything as successful as our parents hoped for. We were just curious kids. It has long been fabled about what curiosity brings.

Dusty books, big libraries, stressing over the amount of literature you want to read with the little time you have, a mental breakdown every few nights, ruddy cheeks prompted by chilly evenings between intermittent swigs of blackberry brandy, antique stores, staring out onto the sunset and thinking: this is where I am supposed to be, crying over dead poets, using old words- without realizing that this was the beginning, and indoctrination to the horror.

These were the evenings and some nights at the Olde spye inn. The Gothic Knights one and all were we.

Long Black coats, evening thunder out at the bay, but no lightning, red wine, blood, forests in winter, imagine a maiden princess lost in the woods- a single melting candle, Our Magister Ludi and his version of Latin; running at the mouth with long rants of cryptic poetry, bones, all of history in your hands, Tchaikovsky, piles of old books, the hour before sunrise, complicated puzzles, The glass bead game, Hermann Hess, true crime, secret diaries. Jim Morrison, and the celebration of the lizard. Jack be nimble, Jack be quick, Jack jumped over the candlestick.

We were just curious kids, really, that was all; just curious kids.

We all met as child strangers. As teens we did not know, we searched around for our own identities. We came from different places, and when we met we stayed united. Almost like the omnipresent demons of this place brought us here. Like I said we were just curious and curiosity was not popular, it was annoying to the middle class; so we dropped out, we formed the Atlas yacht club.

Key harbor opened up its seascapes across the bay overlooking the Jetty; as I have said, I think I might have mentioned at any rate… it is exactly that existential horror that brings my friends and me back to this pitiless place. Can the soul of a place be so cursed that nothing grows there? A town, a loch, a harbor, or even a jetty for example; our jetty, the others, and myself? What of that Rock island that lies beyond barren of seaweed, or crustation; never do seagulls fly around it, only the mosquitoes flourish. That cloudy mist is so dense that it always looks like undulating dust quivering over the stones… that tiny spot off the horizon.

The sea is filthy with its unholy decadence down to the rocks and weaved in shells that bury its secrets; the gravestone epitaphs of lines and circles embellishing its dank dark decay. From the bell tower, you can look across the shimmering glass carpet of a briny substance until your eye stops at the murky tide around the caverns.

On those nights you could feel the calling, those eyes that seem to be always looking up to you from underneath, shallow and below. Back in the chambers, not treasure or reward, a bounty of any kind, only the filthy history riddled with secrets and abominable deeds.

The Atlas Yacht club was an escape for us. A journey into the mind's eye where no holds barred discussion lent us the freedom into flights of fantasy and introspection. Each one brought his particular talent and daemon to the table for resurrection. The Magister Ludi John Morris, for example, was forever interested in ethnography and myth, his love of symbols was no surprise to anyone that he was to pursue his dreams; nightmares as well, and embark on a career as a sociologist of some sort wanting always to know the history of things and what they meant. Even after the horror, he never lost his grit.

Sean Anthony our whimsical artist and sculptor…had a true lust for life always living off the land, building fires, and caring for the weak and infirm. He was saintly in his passions always feeding the animals and befriending a local vagrant. Monk-like in his aspirations; his simple whims he brought us Hobo cooked meals over open fires and coffee brewed in a soup pot that was ladled out and drunk from the dented tin and chipped ceramic cups that we salvaged from scattered ruins. It was no wonder that the horror had very little effect on him except that it might have driven him a bit more eccentric without his being fully aware of it.

To the rest of us it was quite clear that with his brew basket already brimming to the rim with eccentricity as it was, any slight addition of more surrealism could bring it to a boiling point, thus spilling whatever sanity might be left him into the ethos of obscurity. Sometimes an open mind into the abstract and absurd such as the mind Sean Anthony possessed could make it difficult or impossible to put things back together once they fractured and reality dispersed. For example, If you took Pop art symbolism and cubed it and then ran it through a spaghetti press, you might get a linear structured Jackson Pollack or maybe a Basquiat- Ha Ha! See how I did that, not bad for a maniac right. Am I right? That is not to say that he did not witness the horror…he did, he merely internalized it and recycled it as art.

And as for myself, I am a writer; to record the horror that was my calling. I have no great success story, I have never written anything that would be popular on the pulp fiction shelf; only that I have survived the horror of this loathsome town, a town that has no beginning just a continuum of controlled evil. It is a story I tell to my chronicler, Doctor Bursar.

I feel cheated and robbed that so much of my innocent childhood was taken from me in those days of my early youth. A boy should be able to walk along the shore and find fantastic mystery on the beach without getting perverted by an ancient evil that he could never understand.

My dark experience with a girl who was beyond her years; a brush with phantasmagoria, inexplicable horror, and love that suspended us both… It was not just I, but Magister Ludi also was imprisoned on a quest, an odyssey that has led him so far from home in his heart and mind that he might never come home, never to be normal again; normal in the sense that other people are normal; to sit on a couch with a loved one and watch TV and order take out… no not the Ludi.

We are objectives of a great painting, we three, The disease of the mind that was Bosch, perhaps (he); Sir Hieronymus hell himself, was affected by way back in the thirteenth century; the disease that ran through his veins found a host in our own Sean Anthony as well, by way of manifest through color fields and frames; unsettling sub —consciousness waves of lines and pigment; and of course there was the creatures. If not for his collective eye and recall, no other record of what they looked like would exist. It was in his torment that he recaptured the horror. Although our meager senses and defense mechanisms permitted us to observe the chain of events differently from one to another, each according to their sensitivity; we could all agree on one thing. At the viewing; what we were looking upon was not of this world. But, strangely enough —at the same time; it was.

9/ Thursday

This is concerning the letter from Magister Ludi. On how we were to meet and come to terms once and for all about what was to be done about this terrible secret we all held as children. It is time now to move on. This was maybe a month before I took it upon myself to burn everything down. It was stewing in me for quite a while I do confess. I should have done it sooner. With everyone gone what was I to do; Aggie a sea hag and Fitzy dead. How we carted him out to the caverns and dumped him there for maenad's to deal with... I was scared shitless I will tell you that. The others were pale and puking, only Aggie sat still and directed each action. But before I get ahead of myself ... so there is less confusion, let me explain about Ludi's letter.

It came out of the blue, so it seemed, but he must have been considering it on it the whole time. We all were in denial about what was to come. No one was at peace. Sean Anthony was living a squatter's life. He escaped to England and was holed up at Earl's Court with some friends selling art in underground communities trying to forget, trying to be normal' or as normal as anyone can expect once you have the horror inside you.

A blood-stained maniac immune to mercy

This was the tale as researched by our Magister Ludi. Our most devout member, dedicated to the truth and history of our rotten heritage. From his notes and journals, he composed. The letter he sent to us each at our own homes distant and far away, our lives filled with the daily activities of normal men. Not content with getting away once with our juvenile crimes and indulgences, the Ludi, had to go back to the scene and confront the horror all over again. With books and letters, ancient manuscripts containing spells, and incantations. What right had he to conjure up the fairytales of wizards and witchdoctors?

It was his letter that summoned me, not just me, but the others as well. It rang almost as a last will rather than that of a cordial calling card. The Magister Ludi was never the cordial type mind you, but this was different, he had changed; grew more frightened than the rest of us, more inquisitive, as though knowledge and keen understanding would somehow save him. But how could understanding save you from evil? Its bitter intent is to corrupt you.

Sean Anthony and I had moved on somewhat, getting away from it all and attempting to start over, to mature as they say, possibly marry and settle down like so-called normal people- the status quo. That was the plan for living I suppose. The rituals were handed down to us from our parents. I was cared for, well educated, filled with hopes and dreams the same could be said of Sean Anthony, Now after countless failures, a letter from the Ludi appears one bright normal morning- injecting new hope for a fresh start of doomed adolescence. You see we never wanted to grow up us three. This was revealed to me in not so many words right here in the shrink ward. I was locked in a kind of juvenile delinquency state of mind that I could never grow out of something that happened in- at the harbor so deep in the inner recesses of my mind that even Doctor Bursar could not pull it out.

The letter went as thus:

My dear friends, I knew you were faithful. You have responded with Godspeed holding to our clubhouse vows as quickly as I would respond to yours; Kudos ye Devil-dogs.

Some years have transpired without you seeing me, may the friendship that has bonded us all these years be fortified and assured by the story I hold in store for you. Though I summoned you suddenly with the code we devised (code "rapscallion") assuring you this was no hoax or friendly meeting. My only wish is to talk to you in hopes that you might listen.

I have reached a point in my life beyond which I cannot go. I can no longer understand things. The last time we saw each other was at the Olde spye eight years ago. It was then that we separated agreeing it was time to terminate our vows to the yacht club and move on; never to speak of the horror. I have traveled extensively since those days to complete an essay on the Phrygian cults; this was the body of my work however I could not leave the history of the Berserkers alone. The idea that I could have lived a different existence or that I could have lived differently(Knowing what we know) has never entered my mind. The knowledge I acquired was so great a find I have to share it with you, my only comrades, or I fear I will go mad. I spent all my fervor on my work I loved a few friends you both are among them. So I am clear; we are not wrong on our assumptions. It is about Aggie also, the last time I saw her she was wearing a long veil flowing from a big straw hat. She sat motionless in that tower. So the being to which I attached my life had a real and individual life all her own. She felt I was looking at her and she turned toward me. I replaced my feelings that hollow sense of loss the best I could with stern gallantry. She in turn looked almost through me with a fixed glaze and a gloom of mourning that sent shivers of icy shards through me. Then she very tenderly smiled. I intended only to stay there a few days, but my fatigue grew greater and more intense as the clock moved on. I should have thought it shameful to give up so easily.

I know Charles that you had romantic feelings for her, I confess so did I. I thought of visiting her so long after your departure I might have a chance. But the feeling of discontent and gross sickness came over me and the sudden nose bleed…I could feel she was sending me off. The distance between her and I could never have been greater. It is no secret I had never wanted her to be part of this thing of ours. I could not separate my study in her from my true feelings that have grown over the years, and now the things we know.

We were content as children with our stories and make-believe demons until she brought in her Horrible mess. It was you Charles who loved her. The horror was there before us. She could not ever really be like any one of us, you must have known that Charles. She must have told you…but that wasn't enough for your lust. The water from the bay had already been stinking from the time I got there. That brine odor that has become familiar to us. However adequate, I cannot expect everyone to share my disgruntlement or Aggies. We will meet then and at the time we agree to I will make my findings known. I am looking forward to our assembly.

As Always John. Your Magister Ludi.

That was the first letter from Ludi; to follow there were biographies and maps of ancient Viking folklore and History… None of which fully explained Aggie or her relation to the Maenads.

The relationship with Aggie was serendipitous. How I met Aggie and her invitation to join the Atlas Yacht Club was purely selfish and self-indulgent on my behalf. I fancied myself in love with her.

Well, on this one fated morning I was walking along the shore, a boy no more than thirteen or fourteen maybe, I can't say I remember all that well, The mind erasing meds they have been feeding me leaves a hole in my medulla medulla. Well anyway, with that being said, I had nothing to do this fine day; nothing to do pushing horse crabs over with a stick and then kicking them back into the bay. The water was rough for a few days. The daily washing ashore of finely ground tidbits of debris and many translucent jellyfish. No treasure, however, no gold doubloons or cool whale bones… just debris.

I looked up and from out of nowhere Aggie was just standing there, a cute picture-perfect girl about my age. At first, I could not believe I was on the beach alone with a girl; like a dream, If I had found a magic lamp on the beach that day I might have wished for this exact chance happening. It is funny how life happens when you are a romantic young man coming of age always hoping for an easy find: The girls, the beach, the summer breeze; snails and pails and puppy dog tails, or some such nonsense.

"Hi." I remember saying, barely in a whisper.

She looked at me half squinting from the sun. She looked past me and then over at the Jetty where the caverns were.

"Hi," she finally responded. One other thing I noticed was that Fitzy's boat was gone, maybe that is what she was looking for out on the horizon.

"My name is Charlie, you from around here?"

"Yes, I'm Aggie, I live over there". She pointed over to the bell tower and quickly turned back facing me. I signaled a sign of relief feeling she was comfortable enough with me to tell me her name.

I am looking for cool stuff for my shell collection. Seen anything?"

"When you live here" you find lots of stuff." She said.

Yeah, I bet, wow, you live in that tower?" That's really cool. I bet you see lots of cool stuff from over there?"

Aggie smiled with a look of approval and a kind of cloud swept away from her face.

"You think so?" Thanks, um, well it's not so great, a lot of people around here think it is kinda weird. They don't like me very much. I am a Cropsey white. That's what they call me."

"What does that mean?"

"I am not sure? "I am descendent from the Cropsey section of Olde Dutch that came here years ago… They were an odd bunch I guess. I have Pirate blood. That's what they say. Seafaring people going back as far as the Vikings…. The berserks have you ever heard of them?"

No." I said.

"I found some books that have been in my family for years. Oswald says I am not supposed to read them, but I do, I sneak it."

She told me that "Oswald was her dad, I thought it strange that her father was called by his first name, but she said he insisted on it, he hated to be called dad, daddy pop, pa… any of it.

"I collect stuff too, I collect mermaid tears." She reached into a small purse she was carrying and pulled out a few shards of crystal glass. Some were round like small pebbles and others were smoothed around the edges.

It is glass that has been in the water a long time, buffed and worn down along the sand; pretty cool right?"

Yeah, I have seen those I never knew what they were I thought it was, pirate treasure ….

No, no…. she said letting go a laugh, "Just polished glass". Here look close you could see sometimes what pieces of bottles they are from. This one has a peps-lettering, it Could be a Pepsi soda bottle- that one is cobalt blue like a medicine jar. Here is some porcelain probably from an old sink."

"That's how I figure them out. See this one is just a finely polished oyster shell, not glass at all".

She told me the seashell story and many other secrets of the sea, so sweet and gentle was her demeanor; almost as if each one of those cracked polished stones she held in her hand were a personal part of her private history. I watched her lips tremble to form words; as she waxed on, I could not help but fantasize about each expression being brand new and packaged especially for my ears only, word for word; never heard before by any other boy. Expressing her humble memories and recollections in truth withholding nothing.

Then as casually as she picked up the shell, she laid it back down at the ocean's edge. We both watched the ripple slide beneath it gently lifting, carrying it out to sea. I suddenly, for the first time, became aware of how vast the harbor was dwarfing me all around; melancholia settled in; sweeping turbulence of nostalgia is the only way I could describe it. It took years for me to formulate and put into words what that spontaneous emotional upheaval was; After thousands of watts of recent electric shock treatments and buckets of meds…my best and only explanation of what I was feeling that day was the serendipity of infatuation… no it was not that at all, My fate was sealed on that innocent beach. It was Love, the eternal kind, the kind you bring with you to the nuthouse.

"Hey, you want to trade? I have some cool shells from the Bahamas I can give you a whole bunch for a few of those. What do you think…? Aggie laughed and could not believe I knew so little about the sea.

"Here take these you can have them, I have lots." She said.

"Wow, thanks, Aggie… I am sure glad to have met you."

We sat and just watched the sea for what seemed to me to be forever until Aggie broke the silence with an invitation that changed my life forever.

"Hey Charles, you want to see something? It is my collection of sea stuff.

"Yeah sure", I said.

"Well, it is at the tower, Oswald will be getting back from fishing I will show you tomorrow can you meet me here early like you did today?"

Okay, Thanks Aggie and thanks for the stones they are cool."

"They are maenad tears… think of mermaids. That might be easier to remember."

Aggie made a friend; friends were not made as easily as mermaid tears and just as hard to find in her world.

With that being said, in all my naiveté I never knew what a maenad was, it was soon until I experienced one. It was the magister Ludi who one day uncovered their secret through his exhaustive studies in Mythology.

The next day I met Aggie as planned, she looked strange a little different from the other day. Her hair was pulled back and tied making her eyes much wider and intense. When she looked directly at me I thought I saw things in them, golden swirls that were scaring me. I turned away, and when I looked back again they were gone. She took my hand and led me to the tower she looked over her shoulder at least twice, before we came to the big wooden door. She pushed it open and a loud creak made me jump. She pulled a string that jump-started a pale bulb suspended from the ceiling. We went through a meandering hallway that opened into a large space. It was a living quarter. The walls were brick and stone with no windows, a wood-burning stove and sink with plates scattered around, cupboards old and wooden like a nursery rhyme, but very clean and orderly. Stacks of food goods and non-perishables placed in rows. This was all so different from my house, with modern appliances and big breakfront windows; I did not know people could live this way, especially a young girl.

I could not help but think how much more she knew about things than I did. "Would you like some milk or something?" she asked.

"No Thanks, I just ate."

The air smelled of spices and old parquet given up from its waxed dusty depths. Undulating reflections off innumerable brass objects were everywhere for every size and purpose: Buckets, baskets candlesticks, rusty graduated window weights of solid iron are what I thought of over the years. But no doubt I have omitted many other treasures.

To the left of the front door was a small oak-paneled room. Drilled into a faux door there was a circle with a metal cover over it, on closer inspection, I realized it was a peephole that looked out on to the yard. There was a handsome fireplace that was picture perfect it gave one the feeling that even at the height of summer a visitor could not be sure a fire had not just gone out. Standing by the open hearth you caught the bitter-sweet scent of wood smoke and ashes, Mingled with the scent of wildflowers that were everywhere in the dwelling.

Another room filled with books and maps here and there, willy-nilly. At the height of this intemperance, amongst it, all something very familiar was lurking behind every artifact, something silvery.

There was something silvery that radiated from the shadows. Something silvery that slinked across the floorboards hugging the corners of the room; passing spiny fingers along with old book covers. So light and ephemeral was this deviation of breath; not even disturbing the book dust one particle.

It was something silvery, like the flashing fluorescence of a Spanish mackerel, momentarily breaching a dimensional surface upon a peaceful inlet; a ripple on the bay, mercury spiraling up a glass thermometer.

It began as a soft and gentle slithering menace altogether sinister in its dryness. Subtle as a cough from an old man's lungs disturbing vapor as curves of smoke lift from a briar pipe bowl; a whiff of Turkish tobacco and damp leather intoxicated the nightshade apparition awakening two ghoulish eyes and then, two more until the room was a sarcophagus of dead things. They were nightshades that presided over this place. I reached for a door handle to secure myself. And there was none, no earthly way to balance me, no inner peace to be felt; a void where my soul once was.

After a moment my trembling subsided. A false sense of peace encompassed over me.

A silver phantom jetted like a projectile as I stood motionless, it made haste through a glass portal. Then another withdrew into the weathered crack of a floorboard, then the last, a sinewy feminine type. It was the only one of the three apparitions that projected my empathy. A Radioactive glow silver misty breath, a contagion of bitterness and sweetness. She-(it), I sensed that it was female, whispered to me. it was a foul creature… "And what was it worth to worry and where did it go?" -That is what it said to me; at once fomenting the scent of pine needles and sweat. A book of poetry falls to the ground; it was a slim volume of ancient cannons. I saw the letters burn into my mind. Fleurs du Mal, it read. I did not understand at the time it was French.

I looked to the ground and could read the title page of another open book, frozen to be clear and concise. The words were upside down but still legible. The script was of a century only the Ludi might decipher.

Moon cursor; a puff of fetid air pushed the page, poorly written words describing a ship were as thus. "An old whore forgotten whose teeth went all rotten and her hair was the color of wet wood and whiskey. On the floor lies a sonnet with her perfume still on it, wet with the tears of a hundred old sailors and me."

A mysterious and romantic way to describe a ship (the moon cursor)-I recalled seeing the words painted on Fitzys's boat at least a hundred times, but never paid it any mind. I thought almost as though it were a love letter of some kind. Even later in years to come, I lay in bed wondering why anyone would write a love letter to a boat. One of the many mysteries of the Moon cursor. As time went on I was to find out. Now I wish I had never known.

I was entranced for only a few seconds but the episode hung on me like transcendental space in time. Then I got the feeling to write it all down, but I have no technique for verse that handicap, however, was to work out to my advantage… You write a love poem like this one and you do not bother with technique. You write it right or wrong infusing everything you've got. But when there is no love in your heart, you search out a technique or how to put the words together. After all, if you want to write a poem beautifully you must know some technique some level of skill, meter, and all the rest, but if you are writing it for yourself it does not matter. It came to me later on over much unrest, that this was a journal. It might have been written as a testament it might have been written out of fear. However, it was clear to me in my juvenile mind at that time, that it had been written a long time ago. All this revelation came to me in the space of a few seconds.

With that, the nightshade's shape changed and she turned into a young maiden "maenad, a flower of Dionysus. She went forth violently knocking over objects, but I could not move, behind me was a door. I heard it open Aggie was there with a harpoon gun and fired it straight into the heart of the daemon. The creature defused into a keilidesope of gastric polymorphic shapes all silver and blue. Only a dull hiss and a faint snicker was her parting sound. I looked in horror at the wall where the harpoon penetrated passing through the ghoul. At first thinking, I thought I had witnessed a murder. So real was the apparition that in a few seconds only the vapor dissipated through the cracking wall. Aggie was there looking at me silently. She placed a reassuring hand on my shoulder, then yanking the harpoon from the wall, she said, "I will explain in a minute just give me a minute." She seemed a loss for words, remote and embarrassed. I soiled my pants, not being the tower of bravery myself.

Aggie fully composed holding the harpoon gun looked down at my wet pants.

"If you want to get out of those wet things I can wash them for you, they will dry quickly in the sun".

I don't know why or how I reacted so robotically but I took off my shorts and handed them to her then while still transfixed staring into her eyes I removed my underwear; she handed me a towel, which I wrapped around my waist. "Well Charlie, she said, you met the maenads."

"I am standing here in a towel what if they come back?"

"Oh they will not today, they are very protective of me"

"You shot one with a harpoon," I said.

Aggie giggled… "I had to show them there was no need for them to worry. If I didn't react quickly they might have hurt you." The nasty female; the one that threatened you- has a kind of girl crush on me." I stood looking around, nothing seemed out of order, the books were back in place. All that remained was a memory.

My clothes dried quickly after Aggie washed them in a slop sink that was in another room. I put on my underwear and shorts and started home. I never thought that I was standing naked in front of Aggie wrapped in a towel and neither of us made an issue of it. My shorts were still wet but the hot sun did begin to dry them just as Aggie had said. We never talked about that again, Aggie and I, nor did I ever tell that story at the Yacht club meetings not till way later after Fitzy died.

Our first night at the yacht club and how Aggie became a member.

It was late summer that is all I remember of the year. I was preparing our space waiting for the others. The waves outside the Olde spye were particularly nasty. A storm was brewing; a perfect night for one of Ludi's stories about ancient mariners and ghost ships. How innocent we were, ghost stories indeed…I think back of it now, how simple and naïve after coming face to face with a maenad and living to talk about it…what is left for me at these simple gatherings?

It was evening the sun had begun to set, clouds were pulling over the sky anyway it was always dark at the Olde spye. I waited for the boys outside, seated on a piling. The seagulls squawked. How loud they were, gathering in loud numbers circling; it was unusual how high up into the sky they were, never dipping into the sea for an occasional treat, never resting on the land around here, and never flying out by the jetty. I once found a cluster of large dead gulls split opened with maggots overflowing out of them; no blood, no entrails or viscera of any kind, just parasitic larvae feasting on the rotting flesh under-belly.

I have to admit I felt invigorated not nervous or creepy at all. I looked up and squinted from the beam coming in from the bell tower and noticed a shadowy figure jogging toward me like a shiver of testosterone ran from my lower spine to the hairs on my neck. I immediately sensed it was Aggie. I had seen her a few times before fetching buckets or carrying things over to the Moon cursor; most likely doing errands for Old Fitzy.

The Moon cursor; now that was a horror in itself, I always felt it was watching us. The obsessive relationship it bore with Fitzy or should I say he bore with it…funny how I just spoke of it as it was human…It did translate to me like a human entity. And Fitzy loved it, or feared it or dare I say; possessed by it. I thought of the poem.

Who cares? I can say whatever I want! I am a loon, aren't I? I am supposed to have my daily speak of jabberwocky and outlandish chatter…one must perform you know. Not in my wheelhouse and Far from it for me to bilk the taxpayers out of their investment for this steadfast institution; The Dunes.

Well getting back to Aggie.

She was wet with rain radiating an umber intensity against the bell tower light. She was not unlike a Wyeth painting. I was excited to have invited her in. I had secretly longed to meet her after watching her one morning by the jetty. I had not known much of her, nor did anyone ever speak about her in the neighborhood. Olde Fitzy and Aggie were just part of the seascape. The make-up of the town, the demographics of Key harbor comprised itself to that of summer rentals and transient tourists; there was no urgency for anyone to pay indiscernible locals much mind. That trait of inconspicuousness transcended throughout Aggie's existence. No one paid her much mind. Even in school, it was the bullies that drew attention to her. It was the popular kids that had an issue with her obscurity, her inability to dote all over them, the lack of competition. They wanted to know more; they wanted to bring her into the fold; even if only to ridicule, to hold her up as a contrasting example, a victim to sacrifice when their shallow teenage glory begins to fade.

There was Chloe Gates for example. She struggled in academics. However, she always seemed to come off like a star. One generation away from white trash her parents did well-selling boating and other sea craft related products supplying the seaboard area. She was an only child, the teacher's pet you might say, who could manipulate and persuade, but never quite getting on too well with the likes of a Miss Renshaw. The butch guidance counselor who could see right through her, however, Chloe was one to put on the dog with Kurt Crowley the academics advisor and math teacher. Mr. Crowley was also a witty pop culture stand-up comic type and hip go-to guy for wayward students'.

Chloe's resentment toward Aggie rested on an academic award that came to Aggie's late junior year. Quite simply, It was Aggie's literary assignment to write a paper about "your town", something you find interesting about it. Aggie blew her away with a paper written about "The role of Pirates and their history in Key Harbor." It was the romance of a high sea, to say the least, and so intriguing that many of the popular boys began to spotlight Aggie.

The boys were envisioning her differently, as a sort of Pirate girl. Even the way she looked and dressed became a notable buccaneer chic. The flowing out of date dresses and bone jewelry caught on in a Janice Joplin kind of way.

Although Aggie was unchanged by her new persona, the hotbed of activity and the sexual intrigue stirring around her was becoming something that Chloe was not about to play second fiddle to.

She immediately Pulled a posse together that would humiliate Aggie once and for all. The bough finally broke when Colin Furlong began showing a little too much attention to the once homely and forgotten Agatha Fitz Oswald. Colin was a good kid, he loved fishing and pirate stories and was devastatingly handsome for a young man. He was goal-oriented and would never be interested in someone as shallow and vain as Chloe Gates.

It was obvious all over the school how Chloe tried to corner Colin into submission; She first offered the velvet glove and when that did not work she came at him with the knockout punch, much to no avail. Of course, the usual cast of characters for this drama all chimed in; the sycophants and toddies that followed Chloe around in small circles thinking out loud how perfect a match Chloe and Colin would be. Everyone on the female ticket pretty much dismissed Aggie as no competition at all for Chloe.

It wasn't until Colin began to show a real interest in Aggie, by asking her out that feathers began to fly. Aggie declined politely and did not encourage his advances. It was then that she was suspected of being a Lesbian and the Chloe crowd turned on her once again. Even Colin began to shy away. Aggie knew all too well she could not bring any local people into her life. The petty performances, the school scene, the tolerance, the humiliation she had to endure was all for the sake of appearances.

She was a maenad. She is but a mortal and only half-human… but a maenad just the same. With a bloodline that was centuries old and a tradition of blood lust.

If the ancient Ones at caverns had known about this flirting with schoolboys, some people in this clique would die.

That is where Amanda Golan steps in for the second shot of the One-two punch. She was a typical low self-esteem high school bitch. One might say she was the muscle of the duo. She attached herself to Chloe in hopes that some of the stardust might rub off on her. And it did, she made the big-time, that gruesome night her body was identified hung out to dry on a needlepoint dock piling thirty- six yards into the bay.

Low Tide revealed her. Her head dangled from a thin sinewy cord attached to the spinal cord, all blood completed drained off. It wasn't reported in the papers, but her entrails were spilled into the tide still connected to her vital organs, just floating beside her becoming a surf and turf entrée for the crabs and indigenous bottom feeders of Key Harbor.

A curious enigma, Miss Golan was Five foot five, athletic build a stellar track and field girl; not the type for mischiefs of this kind.

A school counselor Miss Renshaw was said to reveal privately to a staff member that maybe with better guidance she might have grown out of her co-dependence on Chloe Gates and found a more defined future for herself. But all in all, with nature taking on its role as judge and jury and family prudence Amanda's boy madness and physical allure led her prematurely into the quicksand of demise.

There had been rumors circulating the school and private dinner tables, about an original Cropsey white; inbred and weird, the center of local gossip, a pariah, she had no religion; some said she practiced witchcraft and called forth devils from the sea. She attended school and passed her tests, but remained always the butt of ridicule from her classmates and townsfolk who of course found every reason to humiliate her whenever they could.

An article appeared in the local newspaper one early morning disturbing our family breakfast. I recall my father gagging on his pancakes huddling over the coffee in a frenzied state that drained the color from his already pallor complexion. He called in my mother who was hanging our swim trunks and towels over the outside clothesline in the yard. He was shouting to her that something gruesome had happened over the weekend at the sisters of tabernacle grounds that was completely out of character to anything that ever happens in this one-horse town. He ran into the yard and read to her privately so I would not hear.

it concerned the church sisters' tabernacle. The dilapidated structure connected to the Belltower that Aggie lived in.

It was mysteriously delicious and a great story for the Atlas yacht club so I eavesdropped intently.

The outside structure, the support, of the old one-time church -sisters tabernacle was a square composite of flat boards and shaker shingles. There were windows boarded up save for one that was now a thick cover of a cover of cobwebs and ivy vine. My mother said it was a hotel for recluse spiders. The door is always heavily padlocked against intruders.

Being that it was built on my Grandfather's land it was forfeited to my family. When the property came to me, I alone had the key; no one, not even the hearty members of The Atlas yacht club had ever been inside. With that being said, the sheer disgust of the place was enough to keep people away. The presence of evil was a natural enough deterrent. Most people could sense it right if they had a soul. One could be pulled into it if they had an evil soul.

My father was concerned because he thought the police might contact him due to the remote connection our family had on the property proper. No contact was ever made. What happens on the constable hook stays in a constable hook.

It all took place one summer of ____ I can hardly recall, a group of marauding teenagers thought it was a good idea to defame the property.

[Let me preface this with some inside information. I found out from Aggie about this story. The troublemakers if you will, were not strangers or interlopers out for a joy ride. Two were classmates of Aggies and the most vicious bullies in the school. The age-old story of some popular troublemakers and their posse gathered together one evening to make sport of Aggie and terrorize her Belltower.

Amanda Golan and Chloe Gates gathered with two other couples along with some beer-drinking buddies. They arranged to meet by the tower yard by the large catalpa tree just around back - behind the bell tower for an evening of Sex Drugs and Rock-n-Roll. It was graduation season and everyone was feeling frisky.

They went as far as almost breaking in. There were yelling and catcalling. Aggie said they called her name several times. She had climbed out along the bell tower ledge and hid out of sight. From her perch along with the bell tower, she could hear everything going on below. They were smashing empty beer bottles against the harbor stones. Drunken slurred voices were coming up from the loose floorboards below.

Eric krimmer was the oldest boy 18 years of age. He came from a neighboring town. He and Tommy loft would come into Key harbor looking for Chloe and Amanda based on their mutual interest in drinking and banging. They were allegedly dating according to the papers but everyone kind of knew they were just drinking and banging. The other couples were strangers in town and just going along for the kicks. They were friends of Eric Krimmer and Tommy Loft. The last thing Aggie heard was; Chloe saying she wanted to kick Aggie's ass. Amanda was occupied by blowing Tommy in the courtyard. The others were out of sight playing music from a radio someone had and smoking joints].

After no response from Aggie, the couples began fornicating and simply quieted down after succumbing to the sedated after-effects of orgasmic discharge.

As they were getting ready to leave the boys thought it good fun to leave their mark by tying their used condoms to the catalpa tree that bends crooked beside the main gate. The catalpa tree was spinney and black. During the day it appeared half dead with huge carpenter bees flying in and out of it. The leaves were huge and fuzzy.

An amazing fact about the carpenter bee, they have a kind of memory radar that gets inherited by their offspring long after that tree is gone the future progenies of the bees will continue to return to that tree looking for a home even if the tree was cut down or in this case burned down to the ground… There have been sightings of the carpenter bees coming back year after year looking for that tree. Years after I burned it down…Call me romantic, but I never tire of hearing those stories

It was a typical evening and everyone did pretty much anything they wanted to, no fear of police intrusion, no one ever goes back there. After a drunken scene of debauchery the gang went skinny dipping by the jetty to rinse off the alkaline residue of bad behavior and to cool off from the damp humid night.

A few of them jibed about what a sight it would be when Aggie came out in the morning to find their contraceptives dangling from the tree.

Some were naked some were not, according to Aggie who was still holed up in the tower, perched on her tower ledge. Aggie spied Amanda partially nude, Amanda reached down grabbing Tommy loft by the Penis and leading him into the dark semi waves of the bay.

There was a buzzing sound that night as loud as cicada bugs; however, they were not that. It was not anything the group could identify; a loud buzzing hum, steady and chilling going in and out like a mosquito circling your ear at night when you are trying to sleep.

What appeared next coming up from the shadows was a cloud moving in from the caverns, slow and ominous. The dull roar caught the attention of the bathers.

"What is that buzzing sound'? Someone asked.

"I don't know; "was the ubiquitous reply.

"I thought I was just stoned, but you hear it too, don't you?"

The slight quiver in their voice indicated something was wrong. A pervasive sense of fear fell over the beachfront.

With that; in the dark of night, horror descended. The only light source was coming from the adjacent bell tower where Aggie sat balanced like a gargoyle waiting for the horror to unfold. The moon was three-quarters full, hardly enough to illuminate.

Something horrible broke from the sky.

Before anyone could blink, three hovering objects the size of Husky bulldogs descended and latched on to one of the girls securing a shoulder an arm, and a leg, just below the pelvic area,- at the meaty part of the thigh, and hoisted her out of the water, kicking and screaming. Within seconds she was airborne carried off to a place of no return.

Still transfixed by the phenomena her male counterpart was next to be carried up. They grabbed him by the shoulders and legs. All he could see were the pointed stinger like features of what appeared to be a mosquito. He could feel more than see due to the almost complete darkness, But still instinctively closed his eyes tight shut as though that might ward off any incumbent horror. The disproportionate claws holding him securely were suction cup in shape with talons that were locking into his skin.

Simultaneously, a phosphoric mist made its way across the water onto the shore where something silvery was transforming. Like wolverines, the figures leaped onto Amanda Goles and tore her open with one wicked slash of a claw. Another ghastly form grabbed Chloe who was petrified with fear and dug into her chest with its free hand pulling out her beating heart...the beast turned to the tower where Aggie was still observing and held up the heart to her in victory as if motioning a symbolic offering for her to partake. The other caught the falling body lifting it to its drooling mouth biting into her side and hungrily sucking at her liver.

Aggie motioned "No" from the sinister shadow; gesturing no communitive effort to involve herself in this ritual. It was a kind of snarky offering from the maenad, who already knew well that Aggie would decline the offer. Aggie was not a murderer. She rebuked the bloodletting. This was the human side of her. These maenads were die-hard vampires. They were around when the berserkers sailed, possibly before that, tales of Bacchus / Dionysus feasted with concubines of maenads in human form. Sometimes satyrs and half goateed elders drank wine from golden flasks.

The wine was what was implied, but the true nectar of the gods was blood. The rituals were painted and described by those ancient artists of Greece and Pompeii; but let me assure you, it was blood they were celebrating, the blood of pagans, blood of senators, blood of virgins and babies.

From the notes of our own Magister Ludi;

"Let the court be satisfied with evidence from the berserks those Hoary Vikings that went into trances to perform their bloodletting rituals to please the maenads."

The local papers said the youths were ripped apart by the jagged stones caught in between the rocks, the girls were somehow impaled on some splintery pilings. When they were found days later, they were covered by a swarm of tiny mosquitoes feasting on specks of their dried blood. The local law enforcement was nauseated by the scene.

It was written up in the local rag as drownings. The tides were unusually brutal that night, small craft advisories had been in effect most of the evening so no one disputed the report that rowdy out of towners got themselves killed skinny dipping while intoxicated. No reports were called in, no complaints were filed about disorderly conduct or otherwise just some kids skinny dipping. Some condoms were found hanging from the tree, the clothes were identified as Chloe's and Amanda's… Some beer bottles were scattered around and possibly some marijuana use. The remains of whatever bodies were found were cremated. Lester Forrester burial and cremations performed the service. Chloe's eyeballs and tongue were missing from her skull.

Later the next day, some parents reported their children missing to the Key Harbor police. Collaborating the find. Yvonne Gates said her daughter was sleeping over at a friend's house and never returned home. That story coincided with Cheryl Goles's story that her daughter Amanda was staying at a friend's house, one Chloe Gates. The police and all other parties pretty much left it conclusive. The boys involved were known as juvenile delinquents with some prior history of misdemeanors.

The speculation on what happened that night is why The Atlas Yacht club kept coming back. These little stories were driving us mad.

I had known that Aggie was a maenad. She never kept it from me. However, she was mortal and it was not easy for her to shape change and she did not always have to have blood as they do. She keeps close watch over the caverns and entertains the maenads but this time it was out of her control. They swept in from the sea wild and angry tearing everyone apart. The trophy pieces they left impaled. The ones reported missing were brought back to the caverns alive for a bloodletting.

The bloodletting was a ritual unique to the maenads. They had a farm of special mosquitoes that are hundreds of years old. The mosquitoes are the size of cats and very lethargic. They mate. The offspring are not quite as big but can kill a large seagull or squirrel or rodent. Sometimes small children are abducted by maenads for the queen mosquitos. When the drone mosquitoes are plump enough with blood the maenads eat them. This keeps them at the caverns so they are not detected by humans on the mainland and do not have to hunt their food. Quite simply put, the maenads are blood junkies, and the mosquitoes are the drug of choice.

However, sometimes small children are abducted to satisfy a ritual performed by the maenads that go back to the Berserks, perhaps even farther, even the Ludi does not know for sure. But there have been writings in ancient scripts dating back to the Dead Sea scrolls. But have long since been disregarded as false Apocrypha written by a cult of defrocked monks in the tenth century.

Ludi does not believe them to be false. He has compared them to some of the writings and maps we found in Aggies wunder Krammer to manuscripts the Ludi has copies of from all over the world and they indeed appear to be valid texts.

A BRIEF HISTORY OF A MAENAD

From the notes of our most dedicated and esteemed Magister Ludi.

Maenads, a female follower of the Greek god of wine, Dionysus. The word *maenad* comes from the Greek *maenads*, meaning "mad" or "demented." During the orgiastic rites of Dionysus, maenads roamed the mountains and forests performing frenzied, ecstatic dances and were believed to be possessed by the god. While under his influence they were supposed to have unusual strength, including the ability to tear animals or people to pieces (the fate met by the mythical hero and poet Orpheus In Roman religion. Dionysus's counterpart was Bacchus, and his female followers were called bacchantes.

Orpheus was later ripped apart by the Maenads on Dionysus ' orders for the depressing music. His head and harp floated in the sea for a while before being found by Apollo. The god cast the harp into the stars and the head was made an oracle at a shrine at Antissa. Special thanks to our own Magister Ludi for the fun facts.

PART 2

It was never really clear what Aggie's relationship to Fitzy was only speculation and hearsay. She stayed in the tower and he on his boat; The Moon cursor. It was only a few months into our friendship I came to understand. She was only a victim of the horror the same as we all were, the only difference being, with Aggie it was difficult to distinguish with whom the horror began and with whom it ended as I have on more than one occasion stated.

I still remember how she looked that day as if she were standing in front of me now. She wore blue dungaree jeans a bit outdated but snug hugging her boney hips. She was skinny in an emaciated sort of way that was becoming to a girl and youthful in a young woman. It became immediately apparent by her overall projection she was not comfortable being either. I motioned for her to come in. After some brief small talk, I could tell she was not comfortable with small talk and neither was I perhaps that was the attraction. She wore a simple tee shirt that might have been a man's undershirt. Most likely Fitzy's… I thought. It was obvious there was no budget for clothes and a debutant sea-hags life does not cater to vain accessories. She wore no obvious bra; her breasts were pointed and perfectly silhouetted from behind the light. As I lit more candles, I could make out the features of her face, from the under-glow of light, she was cut and sculptured. Thick full lips of Dutch peasantry and ginger softness illuminated from underneath the pale translucent coloring Of Celt ancestry. She had been observing us: Ludi, Sean Anthony and myself)from the beginning of our Yacht club meetings, and unbeknownst to me she had been watching me since my first arrival to the beach. We shared a mutual attraction that was clear from the get-go.

There was gray area in Aggie's life, one I did not fully understand until years later. It was her attempted suicide that began her life. It was being born again in reverse if you can understand. Aggie had never known just how different she was. If Fitzy knew he never made it an issue, hoping perhaps it would all go away; not manifest into horror; she was after all mortal and mostly human. A bastard child I suspect from unholy intercourse between a mortal and a maenad.

Aggie had told me tales of them; The maenads. How they could shape change and sometimes look very human. They once were Human, but that was centuries ago maybe even at the birth of the world who knows. But some, rare as it is unconventional, to say the least, can shape change into forms of angelic beauty…legend speaks of (According to Ludi); these Maenads share a bloodline back to the fall of Lucifer and his first progeny on earth. These original demons were quite beautiful or gave the illusion of it. The composite psyche or emotional map that was given them was comprised not of wisdom and goodness but vanity because of the rules put in place at the time of the fall. It was not (time) as we measure it, here as mortals, but a continuum on a quantum scale created by the master of the universe to complete his plan.

This theory was conceived by Ludi one evening, that Fitzy might have mated in his youth with one of these attractive shape changers and the result was Aggie. Think of it as "the blues had a baby and they called it rock and roll". He said We were too startled to find any humor in it the comparison.

A STUDY IN GRAY

From the journal of Aggie:

Note to self … Saturday 6:45 A.M. Dog mouth beach

Looking back at it now, I can't help but feel sorry. I apologize for giving you love so strong it hit you just as how the waves crash into the shore — beautiful yet so overwhelming in its strength. I feel sorry you don't feel deserving of it, so you did what you do best: pushing those who love you away. Most of all, I feel sorry for myself. I apologize to my younger, my immature self for letting her believe there was something so totally wrong with her that she could offer her entire heart on a silver platter and you'd still refuse it. I feel sorry I let her (my silly self, all too human self,) believe she was too much when you just couldn't handle her in all her being. Because she wasn't too much, you just weren't enough.

The cliffs are small; they pull off to the side of the horizon forming the jawbone that rises from the salty depths appearing as jagged teeth jutting forth from the great mouth of the subterranean cavern.

These cavities of sand and seaweed are submerged at high tide indicated only by the subterranean turbulence of twists and swirls juxtaposed along the dark jetty. the fact that time passes and things change and people leave and you can only go back to a place emotionally, however, you will never really be there again............... I don't understand how we are meant to endure that.

Their fins and little hands are feminine. Sometimes they are pretty like(not appealingly pretty, in a different way:)sort of like how a fish can be cute, kind of…They want to kill Charlie but I won't let them. Why are they so jealous?

xo/xo/xo Aggie.

I keep Aggie's journals with me and I have read them a thousand times.

This place which she speaks of where she almost died became my special place. This is where we would meet. It was magical. She tried to drown here, tried to end it all by casting herself into the smashing surf, but she did not know she could not drown. Even against his soul fetching turbulence.

The locals refer to this unholy formation of mandible fangs and projections as the Dog's mouth. It was a name that was put in place by the early merchants and seafaring folk that did trade here well over two centuries ago. The harbor was shaped like a key, due to the natural land formation merchants were blessed with easy access to ports as I previously mentioned.

The harbor runs down from the mouth of the channel to the river they call Nava sink. Legend had it that the colonists would gather to discuss markets and contraband prices; further up north, as far as the eye can see, it continues until it finally empties into the Hudson. From there only a seaman's charts will bring you into the ocean.

More importantly, from the shore, a lighthouse bridge was constructed to keep a keen watch for pirates and bootleggers. Later during the Revolution, it doubled as a lookout for British ships that could be spotted coming in from great distances.

The rock formation extends to a sandbar easily accessible by small boat or marine craft. It lifts its fearsome haunches about halfway above the sea between the beach mainland and the caverns. And can be seen only at certain times of the day providing the fog clears. The fog never clears; it sometimes becomes less cloudlike and translucent allowing onlookers a brief glimpse of the horrible dog's mouth.

This is where eventually Fitzy would be dumped.

The jetty is what Aggie walked out on to that drizzly morning.

Between the unpredictable currents caused by the erratic breathing of the caverns and the claimed disappearances of curious visitors, the dog mouth has taken on folklore status akin to the Devils triangle or some such famous place. Although the myths and superstitions attached to the place are small in reputation the overall folk law is compelling. The power it processes compared to other famous sites of interests is punitive. Most of the horrors are never reported.

"That which dies in Key Harbor stays in Key Harbor."

Chalk one up for the Gothic Knights of the Atlas Yacht club; Sean Anthony tagged a wall one night marking a place at the Olde Spye inn. What we needed for our cabal of warlocks was a photographer, not one photo was ever taken. No one will ever believe any of this ever existed, isn't that so DR. Bursar? Not based on my insane testimony, according to you, I just needed some sort of narrative to burn a historic section of town down. Shits and Giggles, you say, I don't think so.

From Aggie's journal,

A great number of suicides take place on the dog's mouth ridge because it is so easy to die there. If you dove into the turbulent water of the dog's mouth you would instantly be sucked into its undertow once consumed you would be thrashed against the spiny rocks and barnacles; nothing survives it, not even sharks come into its orbit.

From the diary of Agatha xo/xo/xo

Note; Thurs. He did not come to the beach today.

I was there. I come to think; my place amongst rocks. I fancied myself as a mermaid at times at home on these stones, breaching like an ancient sea creature, no one to judge, free with the wind and tide to sing and act out as I please.

Free from Oswald, the belltower, This petty town, and all its prejudices.

It was here no one came for fear of its danger. But I felt solace here, to roam free.

Tues.

I paraphrase, from a tale told to me by John Morris one night at the Atlas yacht club.

In Homage to these living stones, it is said that a Viking chief, a Berserker, was exiled to these caverns in the eighth century by a jealous warlord that fancied the Berserker kings wife. This unnamed Berserker is fabled to be the first true visitor to the not yet named American shore, before even Leif Erickson.

It is a legend, that he (this fierce king) disarmed and beheaded one of the three Viking warriors that brought him to the caverns and shredded the other two before the eyes of the chieftain responsible for exiling him and stealing the kings' estranged wife.

It was known throughout the pagan seas that three Vikings were no match against one Berserker it was foolish for this warlord to attempt an overthrow.

So angry was the King, he smashed his sword into a jetty stone and blood poured into the ocean, swearing vengeance on the chieftain and his crew... So much blood fountained from the stone that it surrounded the chieftain's ship. Horrified and spellbound by this curse the chieftain commanded his crew to row relentlessly with Godspeed to escape the blood before it touched the ship.

From out of the blood-stained sea rose silvery figures. The tide itself began to stink with the putrid smell of death. As though lightning had struck, the silvery avengers bordered the ship slashing and tearing at all with an equal vengeance until not one crew member was left standing. The entire craft was returned to the murky sea, to float alone and soulless; its crew members and chieftain slaughtered at the helm.

The Berserker King abandoned and left to die on the caverns only to watch his ship sail away. He was never to see his beloved wife again; this was his punishment for striking the stone and disturbing the maenads were they rested.

The last thing he was to see as his ship and dead wife sailed away was the name scrawled across the side of the ship, that he painted on to its broadside; with his own hands in human blood was the unholy epitaph MANEN FORBANNEISE (moon cursor).

Aggie xx-xx

Thurs.

I am no stranger. One day I will be cool and sexy, and well connected, I will live in a big city… No one will know I am Cropsey. I will be shrouded in mystery and live in a swank apartment. Like those girls in magazines. Everyone will be in love with me. But for now, I have peace here, and if the water swallows me today I will show the maenads they cannot drown me. I will be immortal.

I disrobe my garments

The cloth shackles that protect me from men and their coveting eyes

-alone to the moonbeams only, I open my thighs.

Mollusks and cockles tie rings on my feet, my ankles and toes caught in a loop of defeat.

Slowly they pull me closer to the sensuous sea.

Half heartily I resist, unable to get free.

Surely to my death, I will be pulled inside, bearing notice to my kinfolk,

The epitaph,

By the sea, she has died.

When one is drowning the events of past life sometimes rush past with incredible swiftness. Many details have not been recalled for years. However, I have not many years in my short life. I sometimes recall events before my present life… am I to be held accountable for that also? My present life forever a scapegoat for the sins of ancient and quaint depravities of those ghosts that lie dormant at the bottom of the sea? Am I to visit in the last seconds of life the judge and jury of useless dread and anxiety.

And some of them have long been forgotten. As I was sinking it seemed all the events of my life were reviewed; from the cowardly awkwardness which had predicted the tragedy to the effect, it would have on my Kinfolk. (if I were to have any kinfolk to name except for Fitzy,)how it would be translated to the others; a thousand small details associated with home, the entanglement of peers and school acquaintances, the embarrassment which would proceed, if they were not to die; to go on wounded would be a fate worse than death. To Charlie, I leave my legacy, my name, our time together.

Aggie

On what I know of the caverns and my mother

A light fog has for always, or as long as anyone can remember settled around the caverns. Science says it is natural steam that emits from some underground hot points releasing the vapor into the air; some leftover volcanic heat from thousands of years ago. Folklore has it, however, to be the breath of a dragon, that still lies buried from a time when the devil's children roamed the sea, pulling whalers in with reptilian arms carrying them off to their murky death; Till one day, they {the caverns} were swallowed by the very sea they ruled; sucked into the molten holes of steaming lava, imploding into the inner earth; mother of life and death sequestering them forever in a tomb of fiery magma. Those eyes that come up from the water they swim so fast.

They saved me. I was not meant to die that day. My blood never feels the cold chill of the water as Fitzy's does. They came up, and I looked into their eyes. There was empathy. I had always felt them watching. I was a child, they cared for me. My mother a maenad, A direct bloodline from the ancient ones I am told. Beautiful, angelic, large glass-like eyes the color of the sky at times, the color of flaming opals at other times. They could become coral pink at the setting of the sun. Her nails were translucent with pink coral hues radiating from beneath. She had the mark of a princess; her earthliness the others did not possess; her features that of a human.

I have one memory of her holding me, I was very young. She took me into the tower and tested me. I must have been an inept student. I must have been more human than maenad she knew I was not immortal... My mother was not immortal. Fitzy told me all about it, years later. The promise was that he would have to tell me. And he was protected all these years... The Moon cursor was his legacy; she alone was the one who protected us just as the Moon cursor protected him. It was her, I believe, my mother (Martha she was called), who possessed it. Fitzy named her Martha, she needed a land name. She was the one who protected us. The maenads were jealous of her; Jealous of her legacy jealous of her bloodline, Jealous of her regal status over them, my mother's vanity could be wicked.

My mother was a Queen. She left caverns to stay with me, only going back for nourishment, only the kind the sea could provide for she could not remain on land permanently, but only in intervals.

Fitzy was terrified of her, I know that now. He did what was expected of him, and he lived. When He died, Charlie, John, and Sean Anthony helped me dispose of him. The plot of how we did it still sickens Charlie to this day.

Aggie, xo/xo/xo

CHAPTER 2

It was years later that I came to have anything significant due concerning old captain Fitzy. It was my nineteenth birthday and feeling kind of blah. I took a ride to the old harbor just to do something different, I had never really gone into the mainland town except with my folks and that was for ice cream or some shopping-related thing with my mom. I never considered checking out the local scene, but somehow having spent so much of my summer youth there at the beach I decided what the hell.

Was it that? I had to ask myself or was it I wanted to go to the bell tower? I wanted to see Aggie after all these years. After he died,(Captain Fitzy), and that last time we all were together, it took all these years to shake it. I never thought anybody was going to come back. But I was wrong.

Ludi and Sean Anthony were thinking of it the same as I had. Even the detours we all took in our semi-adult lives nothing was more exciting than pulling the Atlas yacht Club together one more time for a reunion. None of us could shake the horror with Aggie as our source of reckoning.

I didn't know what to expect I didn't know what had become of her. My last letter was not returned. As far as phone, forget it, not one of the Fitz Oswald's was that tech-savvy… There were Pennsylvania Dutch more computer literate than Aggie. Nothing could have prepared me for what I was about to discover when meeting Aggie again for the first time in almost twenty years.

When I first arrived at the cottage, My summer home now that my parents Betty and Ed don't use it anymore; they packed up and went to die in Florida, at some God-forsaken place called "Canopy Trails", the ancient Caucasian burial ground for old white retires like my folks. I remember the brochure they brought back from the realtor, waving it around all happy-like; my Dad dancing around the room like a damn fool singing the jingle; "Leave it all behind and set your sails, You can live your dream at Canopy Trails "We all sat and watched the CD featuring the enmities Canopy Trails offered along with a robust club-style community. It featured what appeared to me as drunken retirees partying on their way to the boneyard.

I pulled in to Lafayette drive, it looked like I beat the rental crowd, all was deserted. The homes looked to be in pretty good shape except for a few that nestled off the back end of dimly lit cud-de sacs, a target for local delinquents to sneak into and drink, fuck and leave their tribal marks in the way of shriveled condoms and empty booze bottles. Someplace to stay warm for a little while, miscreants.

I went inside and tossed my duffle onto the couch, all the furniture dusty and covered up like in a Daphne Du Maurier novel; cozy after a long winter's nap. The scent of dead air hung in the furniture and doorways. I always liked that smell; oily and dark. It was a complex aroma of shake cedar and coffee. My father used to put fresh coffee grinds in my mother's old nylon stockings, and then hang them around the attic and cellar, The grinds absorbed excess air moisture preventing fungus and dry rot. My old man loved all those little Yankee Doodle tricks, passed on from new Englanders still in practice to this day, at least to pseudo traditionalist and wanna-be colonialists like my dad. I never understood that about my dad; why he did that shit, he was always trying to be like a purest Anglo Saxon. Mr. Quaker Oats. I think it was from the industry he was in being forced to listen as those trite hack salesmen wax on about Martha's Vineyard and Nantucket weekends every summer. I suppose he thought he was missing something, being a new Jersey, city guy and all; working his way up from the streets and all that tripe, or maybe he was truly romantic, hard to believe, but worthy of the benefit of a doubt. Maybe I never really knew the old man that way; He was always just dad, no real personality no past no future… just dad not even a flesh and blood man an individual, just Dad.

My Mom was a little wacky that way too sometimes always making pies from a supposed colonial recipe with all kinds of seventeenth-century shit like rhubarb and mince-meat. I swear, if George Washington ever came to our house my old-lady would have tried to bang him. Mark another one up for old George; He could have slept here too.

The electric power and water were turned on last week so the room immediately filled with light when I hit the switch.

I was holding in a piss that could shame a racehorse, all the while navigating back roads to avoid the weekend traffic. I must have hit every bump and pothole seen and unforeseen sending my bladder and kidneys into what felt like a renal shutdown. When I finally tried to pee it took forever coming forth from tightening up so hard. I should not have been popping beers the last hour and a half of the ride; proof once again I am not one of those juveniles that I ridiculed a moment ago, my spirit was willing, as always, but again, the last laugh was always with them as long as they are young and have bladders that can hold a gallon of urine as mine used to. Now I occasionally piss blood, not good.

When all my sanitary needs were finally in order, I thought it a good gentlemanly thing to have a drink at the local Gin mill. How bad could it be? The rest of the Atlas yacht club would not be arriving until tomorrow so let me at least unwind before I make things ready for them in the morning. With each assigned his room, we can prepare for our meeting. I called for a Campbell's cab that is a local livery for the area and waited patiently for my pick-up outside. I stepped out onto the unpaved road and forced myself to look afar toward Constable Hook. The Belltower loomed, I am certain a light passed the window; an old Scottish nursery rhyme passed through my head. (Wee Willie Winkle runs through the toon,
Upstairs an' downstairs in his night-gown,
Tirlin' at the window, crying at the lock,").

The air began to take on an oppressive heavy musk as the brine from low tide washed up on the harbor side shore…It is there. I felt the presence; it was there.

The sun was going down, the jetty and caverns were still visible by crepuscular light as always. In the evening a fog appeared to be resting over the sunken caves. But I know it was not a dreamy fog but a swarm of mosquitoes; the largest, most thirsty, bloodsucking vampires anyone on the mainland would ever encounter, if they got too close.

The taxi ride was a bit rickety. I could see from the cabbies face he thought it a bit odd I would be going through constable hook. We were quiet the both of us; he for reasons of curiosity and suspicions of me; myself because I was studying the side view mirror that came into my vision from the back seat. We made a turn through some mud I could hear it splash the tires. To the left of the road was an old shack structure with a woman standing outside. She had denim trousers and a moth-eaten woolen cardigan her hair was up in some kind of bandana. The shack was dark except for a dim bulb that hung out front over the porch. A sea hag I thought… a living breathing sea hag. What could her life be like?

The metropolitan area is back there somewhere, somewhere in that rearview mirror. I could hear the dull faint murmur of a foghorn, the tugs coming in from the east; most likely imagining it. A brief reverie of the New York Harbor I left behind. The only vessels around these ports are at harborside. Charming little fishing boats and private sails docked in the marina, folks who had some money, most likely inherited. There was an old wives' tale around these parts. If you stay in the room you were born in and get a municipal job eventually everything your old man worked for forty years will be yours. There Might be some truth to it. I have been seeing some local fellas that have been farting in the same couch cushions their whole lives… No wives no credit cards buy everything cash; they fish every day.

Being around water most of my life, The northern new Jersey industrial side of New York Bays and Harbors, and then later the southern coastline of bucolic villages along the Jersey shore for which I speak of now; I have become familiar with the sounds. If you listen intently from the open porch of the old spye inn as I have, you can hear the evil. Three tones: the first, a hiss of the serpent as it breaks forth from the north wind. Then a dull bass rumbling like that of a low piano key or a cello (E) note rustling up from the core of somewhere as though the whole of the harbor was hollowed out. Sometimes a mural of clouds in the sky form around it like a great viola allowing the rumble to persist to a crescendo. Then a soft treble surrender, a rebuke against the thunder. A softer pitch luring the foam back to the sea. (jouissance). Back to the sea, back to the caverns.

Springing up from the Old Spye road is the bell tower the last remaining piece of firm foundation left of the church.

From here on in, I can't make this normal-too many broken parts.

I must admit I thought myself special being witness to this. A young man, with a heart, yearned for the romance of the open sea; "Call me Ishmael", motha-fucka!

The taxi pulled up to the tavern, The Anchor Inn; quaint. I got out, paid my fare, and left a generous tip. I am always uncomfortable at this juncture of the transaction because I can't help feeling a snarky resonance escaping from the driver's toothless smirk. Experience with this type of individual has taught me that my gratuitous gesture could have been interpreted in two ways. One; the driver thinks I am a city boy on vacation who throws money around like a big shot, or two: a city-slicker prick who is patronizing a lowly cab driver while silently entertaining the thought that all taxi drivers around here hump their sisters. I, however, did not try to come across as any of those things; but if I had to guess…

THE TALES OF BRAVE ULYSSES

I was two beers into the void of the night when the cadaver next to me opened up when I told him I knew Old Captain Fitzy from Constable Hook. He was an old grim paunchy solid type, dressed in a plaid cut off shirt and worn overalls. He constantly mumbled to himself, whether anyone was listening or not. I asked if he was still around," Capt. Fitzy", knowing damn well he died. Unbeknownst to my fine well-oiled acquaintance, I was one of the co-conspirators that helped dispose of the body, along with Aggie and the other members of the Light fingered five minus two-gang, Sean Anthony and the Magister Ludi.

So he went on…

"1898 ww1,ww2 we built that bridge spanned across that little stretch of the jetty from the old spye to the island they now call dog mouth, if I ain't seen it myself I would not go with it-no one was safe then. Big air borne things-shaped like sub-marines; kept dem' bottled up in those caverns they did, cut me thrice if I am lying'. we built that bridge not soon after the hurricane swept it away… ww1,ww2 whole team of fancy fellas, not Government ya know, no one knows who they wern-warned us away, that was 1898.

Me and Fitzy we stayed behind; hid out in those caverns-he- he, not without scars my friend, not without scars. Sumthin bit Fitzy got him the fever, don't know what brought him back to health, Thought he was a goner fer sure; never spoke a word as promised…but then soon I got the fever-Healed up too, like nothing ever happened-never got sick again after that, can't explain it-not Fitzy neither…I used to get the grip in my chest every winter, could but hardly breath when the grip comes on ya- every winter like Thor pounding your chest with a hammer, right around the winter solstice. We was fishing for tuna then' leviathan yellowtails come up from the south; tails so mighty they snap the aft clear from the boat. I scraped ice from the mast in those days every winter since I was twelve. I ain't never got the grip again, oddest thing. But then many things got strange to us in dem days that were right before the awfulness.

Old Margaret, she went mad you know all the folks around here know it- or heard bout from legend being passed on. Ain't much said about it nowadays; reckon most folks want only to get on with their lives not thinking about the dreadfulness of dem days…with the storm and all. Folks know it- old Fitzy hauling her off to that tower- the awfulness- ain't no one spoke about it; taint no one's business what a man does with his wife…in that tower she spent her days' poor old girl locked up in that bell tower ain't never spoke a word just watching out that winda' day an night, pretty young thing she was in her youth-the Old sea hag. He made her that way ya know… I knows it, damn the whole town know'ed about it in those awful days.

HA HA…ca-ca-can't say I didn't carry a fancy for er. Like most young men round ere' But after dat day… no more…nothing left but a sea hag/ watching just watching waiting for the awfulness." Martha had a child… Agatha."

With that barkeep lifted a brow to some able-bodied men sitting at a corner table. Two of them rose in unison coming up behind the old man as one the buried one grabbed the old-timer in a friendly bear hug, lifting him off the stool and carried him to the door the others laughing in a shared camaraderie. "Let's go mittens your old Lady is looking for ya". The hulking man proceeded to carry him to the door where the other escorted him home.

The barkeep returning his gaze to the empty seat removed the old man's glass and any evidence of him and cast me a sideways smile as one does when covering for an embarrassing episode.

"Sorry mister, I hope that old mittens weren't too much a headache for you. We around here are used to his ravings, however, if you are a stranger here, it might be disturbing —all that mad jabbering. He is our local archive you might say; not a very reliable one as you can hear. He is an old salt from back in the day. Mittens we call him because of those hands. Have you noticed them? Big as baseball gloves they are; from years of pulling on those boats.

Back in the day, he could place four fingers into a high-ball glass much like the one you are drinking from, and stretch them out until he shattered the glass. Powerful man he was.,

With that, a watery patron chimed in from the other end of the bar, "Remember that time when those two biker fellas came in here looking to stir some trouble you remember that Karl?

"I remember." sighed back the Bartender in unison with some other head nods and utterances.

"Mittens had his name on the chalkboard next up for a pool game, when this biker fella, erased mittens name and put his own up there. Well Mittens wasn't about to put up with no foolishness, some words ensued, and Mittens grabbed that fella by the neck and pret —nere lifted him off the ground dragging him to the chalkboard squeezing until the fella scribbled mittens name back on that board just short of his last breath. The other fella came up close and mittens just said; "Be still brother or your next." He let the man drop and he hit that floor solid. That other man picked up his friend and carried him out...

Yep, that's about what happened Karl agreed twisting with a nostalgic nod. The bartender turned back to me and continued his story.

"Well, that's our boy last of the true old salts around here."

"Mittens lives up the road."

"In that shake board shanty, you might have passed on the way through here. The wife lets him wander out now and then and he comes right here, has two beers a shot of whisky, and leaves or she comes to get him. His third wife you believe it outlived them all; a living mystery to most folks around here even to the old-timers. No one can figure out how old he or she is. Only Captain Fitzy and himself remain from that hurricane of some years back he was talking about... way before my time. New generations just keep coming up, strangers move in and out and no one ever thinks that much of old Mittens and the Captain. Folks just think of him as old salt, a piece of the furnishings."

"No one pays him much mind. But he is old, very old I have been working here at the anchor inn just for 15 years and he was as old then as when I started; the same as he is now…never appeared to change".

He just rants on with the same old stories every day; dementia I guess. Out of the original three from the time he speaks of, only the Sea hag died. That is Captain Fitzy's, wife Martha. We suppose it was his sister some folklore says it was his wife…he and Martha had been shut —up in that old abandoned plank board church you see over by the harbor. Captain Fitzy buried her right outside in the churchyard garden. Her grave is designated by the Makeshift tombstone cut from shark bone by the Captain himself. Man of many rituals Captain Fitzy is. He rebuilt that Moon cursor crawled inside one day and never came out. He stays in that boat and no ever sees him… if he ever dies the only way one might know is if his body decays enough to let off a morbid stench, prompting the town to most likely burn the whole church and every memory on it down, before anyone is likely to go in and give him a proper burial, You see Captain Fitzy was by no means a God-fearing man; in fact, as I mentioned him to be a man of many rituals; some of which might not be of this world.

"I thought Fitzy died, didn't you say…"

"Oh. You heard a lot of things tonight, my friend, maybe too much. it might be a good idea if you finish your drink and head on back to wherever you are staying' I'll call you a taxi… ah never mind there is your driver now… "Hey Colin, how about giving' this young man a lift back to where you found him?"

The weirdness of this conversation and the steady heave-ho left me no alternative but to leave peacefully, it was clear that for whatever reason they wanted me gone. A large burly fellow sort of leaned into me shoving me off. As I walked away escorted by this cab driver I felt their eyes watching me go.

The ride home was not that much better. Colin was fish eyeing me the whole time. Finally, he broke open with an opening line. Maybe wondering why I was so curious about Fitzy.

"So, what do you think of our town?"

(An odd question I thought. How did he know where I was from out of town?)

"I've been here before, my folks have summer property on Van Buren; I have been coming here since I was a kid."

Then he burst out in exclamation.

Yeah, Wait! I remember you, I thought you looked familiar... the Conliffe kid, damn if I remember your first name,

Charlie." I said,

"Yeah, that's it. Charlie."

"You remember me? Maybe not, I lost a lot of weight- I was the fat kid, Colin."

I failed to say I could remember him, and then slowly it came to mind as these things sometimes do. But, it wasn't the weight loss that threw me. It was the face. He was the good looking kid, my mom used to always say should do cereal commercials. Time had not been kind.

He was gaunt and bald, grotesquely unattractive. It looked as though there might have been a mutation taken to the side of his face. Teeth uncared for in a bad way. Could this be the same Colin Aggie told me about? The high school face Ace that all the girls dreamed would ask them to the prom. What happened in all these years? This stud was supposed to have potential. Too much time in the basement I guess.; never moved on. Dreams get stale quick around here.

"Colin, sure I remember, we were briefly acquainted I remember. The red bicycle..."

"Yes that's right now I have a yellow cab, still steering. Ha."

"I joined in with a friendly chuckle to indulge his dim attempt at humor".

After my cold experienced at the tavern, I wanted to salvage at least one social achievement before returning home. I could tell he was pouring on the old school charm.

"You went out to sea with Fitzy I recall; you knew Aggie. Strange girl, she turned out to be, that Aggie. Like a pirate. She always liked pirates I remember from High-school.

"Really; I often think of her." Whatever became...

She became an old sea hag up in the Belltower after Margret disappeared. That was her Mom died or disappeared, some say she ran off headed south no one knows what became of Margret. she never came out much, she and Fitzy ran the fishing boat, the moon cursor.

(What my old pal didn't know, I had been back to visit Aggie many times over the years… Margaret tried to make a go of it on land away from the maenads. We witnessed the Horror together Margaret and the moon cursor is one. The Maenads made an example of Margaret. According to Aggie, a maenad could live on land for only a limited time but each time they go back to sea to rejuvenate they age a little more. They age very quickly out of the sea. If they are mortal as Margret was they can begin to wither very quickly over a few years they become haggard, although sometimes physically fit they can waste away. This is the sacrifice Margret made for Fitzy and Aggie, she chooses to sacrifice her youth and beauty for them, knowing that she would wither away in that tower.

I am not sure what happened but it was not pretty. It may have scarred Aggie permanently. It put her in a cationic state that I found her in on that awful day just before I burned everything to the ground. It was easy I lifted two five-gallon jugs of gasoline off the moon cursor spread it all around and turned everything Halloween orange, But before I get ahead of myself There is more about Fitz's death.)

This Lad Colin was sugar-coating it. Maybe on my behalf of me being a transient in town, or the suspicion everyone normally has about people poking around asking questions concerning slipshod the history of Constable hook. With that being said, it was not likely I was going to get any information from him that jerk-weed Colin or any other Yay-hoo from Key harbor that night.

We exchanged good-byes, said we had to get together for a drink, but I knew it was never going to happen. I tipped him again, only this time, not as generously as I had before.

I let myself into the cottage and watched from the window as he pulled away. The less they remembered about me around here the better. The night runs to the caverns with Fitzy and the tower trysts with Aggie was enough to take on.

I know about her slow decline in hagism. The cationic state was a study in gray for my memoirs. Once, upon a time, when I was in seventh grade at P.S. number four grade school back up north. At the school I attended as a boy, the class had an end of the year field trip to the Metropolitan Museum of art. Up until that point in my life,

I have never seen a real painting before, painted by a famous artist. Well, there was on display some artwork by the famous American painter James Whistler. He did many seascapes and depictions of early American life. There was one set of paintings that stood out for me more than the others, mostly because of its folklore. It was called, "A study in grey". It was an old woman sitting in a wooden chair with a long black dress, profile view staring straight ahead at nothing really, just posing. It frightened me.

The person who was curating for us mentioned that it was nicknamed Whistlers Mother. And the joke stuck, till this day, but the real name for it was, a study in gray. When I saw Aggie that day for the last time, I thought of that painting immediately; the study in grey. And saw in black and white the pain that was painted on Aggie. Everything was produced in black and white; heaven and Hell, with tertiary greys representing purgatory.

It was the only way it could be. There was no room for color any longer in her world.

Let me tell more about Captain Fitzy, about that unholy night at sea. And the night Fitzy died.

His name was Captain Oswald Fitz Oswald. Only Aggie ever called him Oswald to everyone else he was Capt. Fitzy with good reason, the name was odd and cumbersome like everything else about the man. How we met and became friends despite Aggie is a blur to me like so much of my life in those days.

It was that turning point summer. I had agreed to meet the captain on that godforsaken night on a bet I had lost at the Atlas Yacht club. This was my tribal rite to passage with the old salts of Constable Hook. I stumbled on to what looked like a Hobo camp; A group of worn old fishermen was playing cards and telling stories outside on the pier by the Moon cursor. but it was a once in a lifetime night of Fitzy entertaining some guests over his christening of the Moon cursor, things were still kind of normal at this time. It was a peaceful time before the boat haunted him eventually driving him mad and before his friends began to die off mysteriously.

The sailors were drunk and I was on my way to The Atlas yacht club, somehow I got entrapped in conversation and I could not get away. Let me just add that these men were like carneys in a traveling show. You could not stop them when they were on a roll. And from the looks of them, some of them might have done major jail time. It was no secret that many cast-outs from societies at lodge took seafaring jobs to hide from bad mistakes and the law.

It took the form of a drinking game I could not win. These were seasoned veterans of staunch debauchery and I was a homely simple boy with romantic dreams of the sea life. It was here old Fitzy compromised my youth and my innocence with stories way too imaginative for me to recall vividly. It was here that I made the deal to meet him that burgundy chilly evening. The moon was bloodshot that I could tell you, and the waves swung in a loose broken rhythm that was all their own. A unique swagger like men of the docks have. Whether attributed to an exaggerated machismo or childhood rickets, they mostly all at one time or another develop an exaggerated syncopated gait. The waves seemed to keep a rhythmic orchestration, shifting fluid stability from one side of the inlet to the other; an entire ballet of moonbeams and harbor lights drunk on the cove.

There were no clouds, only mists that twirled in arrangement from above the harbor to the horizon. Anyone else I suppose might see this as a setting of the most romantic kind, but not I, not that evening when Old Fitzy took to the fancy of telling me his secret horrors. In exchange for my soul.

I must admit I thought myself special being witness to this; myself being a young man with a heart yearning for the romance of the sea? I did not tell Aggie anything of my maiden voyage to the caverns she would have been furious. She had warned me about those characters and especially about Fitzy. I had won his confidence that night. He left us alone Aggie and I and for that she and I were grateful.

I skim through magazines and clip photos of pleasant places I would like to go if I ever get out of here; (The dunes for Loons I mean); not likely. I will probably never see the outside world again unless I escape.

I have magazines on travel and real estate; country living, and Your coastal companion, to name a few; all feature the best fantasy living with glossy print layouts of windows overlooking the loveliest scenic prime living that shorefront property has to offer; wicker chairs, and abandoned hammocks. I would be unfortunate if a restless maenad came ashore one evening and ripped your lover's guts out then dragged them into the thirsty sea…you would never hear from them again. How sad.

I did try to burn down a whole historical section of a bucolic seaside community. It did appear cottage core to the innocent eye, I did burn it down. My reason? it was Evil.

This is where Doc Bursar rolls his eyes at me in capitulation. You see, no one believes my story and those who know it to be true wish I would just shut up about it.

A visitor could very easily be taken in by the clever Americana folk feel that endears places like this to the simple and well-adjusted; as they should. A soul should feel the immortality of a gentle breeze or the willow-the wisp cloud formation.

The cliffs as previously described from the east side, on this site, however, the other side of the key forming the beach on the west side are also granite. They pull off to the side of the horizon stretching out a way into the bay, a kind of jetty, not man-made, jagged, and dangerous. They form what appear to be broken teeth that spring forth from the great mouth of the caverns. The caverns lay mostly submerged at high tide filling with twists and swirls, foaming around the jetty mouth like a rabid canine jaw described by the locals simply as the "Dogs mouth". There is a shallow inlet at low tide that, if you can manage a boat through, it will bring you to the caverns; if you can endure the stench of death and foul decay.

No one travels it anymore, even Fitzy, who's unholy commitment to feed those things beyond its gates with buckets of bounty, had stopped cold. The old man just couldn't take it anymore. That was his last trip alive there. There was one more for him, not one he was to remember, for us it was our maiden voyage across the River Styxx; that was my last excursion.

Yes, he took me there once, I had always wondered where he went with his sinister cargo he said fishing and crabbing but one had to wonder. He had a cold box under the wooden seats where he stored the chum that was baitfish for fishing. So he said. Well, we went out fishing one evening after we became friends he knew about me and Aggie and was okay with it, besides he needed me to be around for what was coming next.

There were many things about Fitzy that did not add up, like why was I safe on the moon cursor but Aggie was not. How was it we went out onto that dangerous channel and floated past the cavern when other small crafts could not? I am no seafaring individual, a landlubber all the way, so much so Old Fitzy laughed, one of the few and only times I ever had seen him laugh, was when I turned green with sea-sickness and barfed the whole cruise. It was not just the turbulent water. It was the terrible stench of the Moon cursor.

One afternoon he was going for a late run. I saw him fill the cold box with bags, they were big garbage bags. Only Fitzy was allowed to handle the cold box that was it. I helped him on occasion with other duties around the deck but never was allowed to hang around the cold box.

Then one day it happened. Fitzy ran offshore for supplies and I was left alone. And sure as shit, I opened the box below. I held my nose and peered into one of the bags and gasped.

It was disgusting, cats and rats and other things I could not distinguish were cut and slaughtered and that is what we were delivering to the caverns. There was roadkill, a deer had been hit by a car up the road, I saw it that morning. I was with my father he was driving us to get groceries. My mother remarked, to call animal control and have it removed from the road before there was an accident. When we returned headed back, however, it was gone.

My mother complimented the township for their expediency in dealing with the problem, but it was Fitzy that dragged it off the road and threw it into the moon cursor for evening delivery.

I remember now how we would dock the Moon cursor by the jetty. Hellish geyser spouts spuming steam up through fissures in the foundation of the cavern grounds, ungodly smells.

Fitzy tossed bag after bag of bounty onto the jetty leading to the caverns. We never went directly into the caverns just at that point. It was important for me to remember what he said, his orders clear and direct. The fog and the mist were outrageous. The mosquitoes were nowhere to be seen. The buzz, however, was low and vibrating somewhere beneath the deafening sound of the crashing waves.

Captain Fitzy onshore at home at the port was comfortable at his leisure. Most of the time he blended quietly and was a part of the scenery, folks would roll up in cars and watch him mend his nets and prepare his boat. Sometimes he would be applying maintenance to the moon cursor other times just scratching his head going over some paperwork everything appeared normal, Just a gentlemanly old sea salt in a picturesque setting, with a lovely quaint bell tower looming behind him. His square overalls and bandana shaded him from the beating sun. His oiled canvas hat brimmed over his eyes so one could never detect if he was looking up or not. He was difficult to give a full description of. He drew as little attention to himself as possible. But folks could not help staring.

There was not much old Fitzy could do about it he would just go about his business; weaving nets, or sometimes painting up the Moon Cursor

The Moon cursor was not much more than an old Lobster boat he had acquired at a fishermen's auction a few years back. It needed some work that he was more than capable of applying and within no time he had himself a fine vessel to help sustain his livelihood.

The moon cursor became a folk tale in itself by the way it was rebuilt so quickly. The badly neglected deck timber seemed to repair itself as Old Fitzy took to shinning and painting it. He worked feverishly day and night sanding and waxing; patching holes it was as though he was caring for a convalescent human being slowly bringing it back to life and luster with the Tender loving care he poured over it. It was not as though the broken vessel had not responded to his obvious love, for it took on an aurora of strength and sturdiness that restored pride to the waterfront when it was finished. So much so, That Fitzy took on an obsession that was becoming noticeable to most folks around the harbor. He moved out of the Belltower and into the Moon cursor and spent very little time in the outside world.

According to Aggie… "it was as if the spooky old boat was sharing secrets with him".

Aggie said that as the work on the ship was closer to completion, Old Fitzy began to change more and more. When he left his makeshift room in the bell tower and began living on the boat. Aggie was left abandoned having the whole of the bell tower to herself. As time went on, Aggie felt unsafe around the moon cursor. Things would happen as she approached it; she felt a genuine sensation that the boat did not like her. It was envy she sensed similar to that she felt at school, whenever she tried to excel in something; a base resentment when the other girls and classmates were teasing her constantly about her clothes and being a Cropsey.

When she had tried to bring a meal to Fitzy as was her routine, the walk –up plank connecting the pier to the boat was always mysteriously pulled away and dropped into the water. She called for Old Fitzy but he did not respond. He peered through a portal and asked her rather cryptically; "Aggie what is it?'

"Oswald, I have your dinner, I didn't know if you were coming home, so I thought I…"

"Aggie! Don't ever come here again do you understand? You are forbidden to come on to the Moon cursor. I will come to the tower if need be and collect things as I need them, Don't worry about me I will be fine. I will check in on you as always to tend to the upkeep obligations… you do not need to worry about that. However, you must never come aboard the moon cursor."

She said his voice had changed and his character was different. As time went on he was not himself. It was as if the boat was draining him. But that is only part of the horror that envelopes this foul place. As I mentioned before, I have sensed it also, as well as the Magister Ludi and Sean Anthony.

It is the phosphines one smells on the fishy water…those horrible mermaids the stench of the maenads celebrating with the corpses they embrace; the caverns under that cloud of mosquitoes.

This was just before he died, sitting in the bell tower looking out over the Moon cursor and the caverns. He left the moon cursor for the first time in twenty years and returned to the bell tower to die. Aggie believes the moon cursor willed him to death for leaving her. He left her emotionally, made up his mind. Aggie said she watched him day after day deteriorate. One day, the last day, she climbed those stairs leading to the bell tower for the last time. There was Fitzy; sitting up in his chair completely dead, head rolled back, mouth hanging open. The window had been broken, most likely by the large Ravens that were circulating the room. They were most likely crows. The morning light was coming in, the carnivorous birds the sizes of cats were perched now all around Fitzy's shoulders and neck pecking at his eyes and throat. This was the last account recorded by Aggie in her journal. She came to get me, It was approaching twilight. I was by the old Spye fixing a table for that evening's meeting with the Yacht club.

Aggie never cried or flinched; she just approached me in her solemn way and said, "Oswald is dead. Can you help?"

For some reason, I was expecting bad news. There was a pending shroud over me all day.

"What can I do?" I asked.

"We have to move him," Aggie replied.

"Come look".

I did I must. When I went to the tower I puked my guts up. There was a swarm of morning mosquitoes all around him. He was drained of any blood and it appears that he was vampirized in his sleep. I thought at once to call the police but Aggie was set against it. The scandal would be awful, not to mention the gossip would be much more than she could handle; the onslaught of questions.

After staring for a few minutes more, I noticed Aggie was gone from the room. I panicked with a fear that held me prostrate. I was about to scream her name when she re-entered the room holding a large rolled-up canvas that looked was probably a remnant of a sail. She did not say a word but went right to work, most quietly and most proficiently she spread the heavy cloth across the floor. We both stood looking at it.

Aggie looked at me with a maturity that frightened me. She had a visage of blank authority that held me powerless. I knew that whatever task she wanted me to perform I was going to do it.

We took Fitzy down from the chair and laid him on the canvas sheet. With both hands and with Aggie's assistance we rolled up the canvas and tied it securely with rope; then waited. We sat nearly trancelike for most of the day never speaking. When I came out of it the sun was going down. I had no sense of lost time and was blank as though reawakening from anesthesia. It would soon be time for the Magister Ludi, and Sean Anthony to arrive at the Atlas yacht club for our meeting. When they did I would tell them what had happened and we would make a plan. Aggie spoke for the first time in hours.

"The sun is going down; It is much darker along the back of the tower. We will carry him to the Old spye and from there John and Dean can help us bring him to the Moon cursor."

"Why don't we do it now? "The two of us can roll him out on a dolly …

"No", she interrupted. There is a protocol. And I am not sure how the moon cursor is going to react."

That statement was not altogether clear to me, but somehow I understood with a deep clarity that was clear to me. No one had to explain, it was just understood.

Remember, I was healthy and in my right mind at this time… not the criminal maniac they say I am now; so this bizarre statement that was completely out of character for young Aggie, was as strange to me then as it is to you my dear listener, hearing it now.

I looked out the window and saw the shadowy figure of someone coming up the dusty road, and recognized it to be Sean Anthony. He had with him some sketchbooks and a backpack. I gave him some time to reach the Olde Spye and settle before I proceeded to meet him and explain all of this. On my way out of the Belltower I was greeted by John, Our Magister Ludi whose barreling baritone voice shook me for a moment. I had not seen him through the shadows. I looked back at the window for a moment to notice what I first thought to be bats, escaping from the tower but then I recognized them as the swarm Of mosquitoes I spoke of earlier…curious I had forgotten all about them as they went about their work. The hum of their song was so comforting I had forgotten they lulled Aggie and myself into our dreamy comas all the day and yet not one had flown upon us for nourishment. I watched them as the grey swarm floated like a puff of smoke back to the caverns. Glowing through them was the nauseous yellow ochre silhouette of a soulless innocent that I befriended on the beach that ordinary day. Aggie, Aggie… everything human inside me broke when I thought of her and what she had to rise above. Reverting my focus from John I ran back to the tower. I had to check Aggie one more time, I was afraid to leave her alone for a second.

I held her close in an impassioned way for that last time. If I had known that was the last time, I would have kissed her and loved her…I never told her I loved her.

I told Aggie not to worry.

"I will be right back. I am going to the Olde spye and to get the guys. They are there I just saw John and Dean,"

I took Aggie's hand and gently kissed it.

"Don't worry everything will be alright we will take care of this."

Aggie nodded yes but looked around unfocused, she was wringing her hands with nervousness. Her eyes were a matrix of light… opal fire, the kind of which I had never noticed before.

On that message of confidence, I took off down the stairwell and crossed over Constable Hook road toward the Olde Spye.

When I entered the Olde Spye Magister Ludi was sitting hunched over his makeshift podium writing something in deep concentration. The haunting music of a song called Nantucket sleigh ride was the bumper music of our Atlas Yacht club by a rock band called mountain. I remember looking at a poster of the cover art for the group we had hanging on an adjacent wall, the words on the cassette were- "Flowers of Evil"; never before had that phrase redeemed more meaning for me. It was pleasant to hear the soothing rhythms, something earthly that could bring me home. The boom box style radio system was primitive by today's standards, it was awkward and bulky, however, Ludi brought it everywhere he went. At the time cassette tapes, players were popular. They were the new thing, and the Ludi was lost in sway of booming bass and staccato drum beats. The Ludi lived most of his life inside his head this was going to be different, a responsibility I hope he can man –up for it. I watched for a moment as the cobwebs vibrated along with the window sills. I lowered the machine and the Ludi turned around with quick panic.

I never described Our Magister Ludi to you. He is what would probably be coined, in accord to the parlance of our modern-day lingo; a long-haired leaping gnome. Later that term would come to be synonymous with a nerd; A bookworm or pseudo cryptic scholar, however, presently the Ludi was still aspiring. Upon seeing me, he began reading from a book of gothic literature, a darkly academic poem, and apothecary. So involved was he in his reading, I could not bring myself to interrupt with the news of the day. The mood was captivating.

He had long hair, John Morris did, it was rust and ochre, round tinted glasses slid down from his nose resting on a slight curve midway from the bridge of his nose. The spectacles I called them, added a circular quality to his already slightly pudgy rounded cheeks. He wore a long coat similar to those the horsemen wore in a Dickens tale and linemen's boots.

"Where is Sean Anthony? I need you all together I have some really weird shit to tell you."

Sean Anthony was on the seaside end of the room looking out toward the bay, Quiet and mysterious, he turned away from the window and turned facing us and morbidly said;

"Someone has died. There are purple ribbons in the sky. See; how they drag across the stratus cumulus, There are also dark halos of cadmium along the western horizon…"

It was not unusual for us to speak like this, We were the Atlas Yacht club, after all, spinning tales and telling stories in period dialect; pretending we held outs to some literary cult, is what we did.

I said in surprise that was obvious to everyone.

"can you read death that way?"

No, of course not, you just look like shit hit the fan somewhere. And you got some on you…"

We shared a sinister smile that broke off into urgency. I shook it off, the eccentricity of these two is more than I could take right now, I was hoping I could get them to cooperate.

I thought it best not to beat around the bush and get right to the point.

"Fitzy is dead. He is up in the Belltower with Aggie and we have to get him down to dispose of him."

My God, how did it happen'? cried the Ludi

"I don't know, Aggie said he went up there to die, she said he knew it was coming."

"How are we going to do this? I mean how do the Fitz-Oswald's dispose of their dead?" Sean Anthony asked.

"I don't know" It is up to Aggie. We have him wrapped up in a canvas sail, someone has to go to the Moon cursor and get a dolly, and there might be one in the shed.

Sean Anthony volunteered to get the dolly and Ludi accompanied me to the bell tower.

"Wait."

"Just in time"…The magister Ludi interjected. "I have something fitting for the evening." He laid down the book he was holding and searched his bag for something, he pulled out a textbook inlaid with gold iconography, and opened instinctively like a minister, to a designated page." I was going to read this tonight for Aggie, she was interested in it the last time we spoke at the last meeting, how ironic I have it now."

As strange as this whole bizarre tale was unfolding, things were beginning to fall into place as if they were carefully scripted. The Ludi read from this leather-bound ancient manuscript a text that was formulated from 800 B.C.

Concerning Viking funerals.

Fadiean writings; Book of the dead.

Viking funerals also involved human sacrifice, as servants and slaves were sent by this means to serve their dead master in the afterlife. The human sacrifice, however, depended on whether the deceased was cremated or buried. For the former, those accompanying the dead would be burnt alive, whereas, for the latter, their bodies would be placed in a specific position to ensure that they would arrive in the afterlife.

Grave goods also served to ensure that the deceased was satisfied in the afterlife. The Vikings believed that if the dead were not appeased, they could return as a draugr (or revenants) to haunt the living. These undead beings could cause much trouble for the living, including crop failure, defeat in war, and pestilence. If a draugr was suspected of causing such troubles, the Vikings would exhume the recently dead and look for signs of undead activity. When a draugr was identified, the Vikings would rebury the body with more grave goods, assuming that the person had been highly respected in life. Alternatively, a wooden stake could simply be used to pin the body to the ground and the head chopped off, to kill the creature.

Volga Bulgaria (in modern-day Russia). A detailed account of the Volga Vikings, including the funeral of a chieftain, may be found in Ibn Fadlan's writing, known as the *Risala*. One of the funerary rituals recorded in the *Risala* is that of a particular form of human sacrifice. According to Ibn Fadlan, a slave girl had volunteered to accompany the dead chief into the afterlife. Before being sacrificed, however, she had sexual intercourse with six different men, to collect their 'essence of life' for the dead chief. It must be pointed out, however, that such a ritual was rare. Ibn Fadlan's description of a Volga Bulgarian Viking funeral may be unique to that area and is not necessarily representative of Viking funerals elsewhere

Sean Anthony said: "There are only 3 of us.
We might have to go twice."
The magister Ludi added," Let's see how Aggie feels about it?"
Only I was not amused. We had a lot of creepy shit to do.
"Lets\'s get on with it."

When we got to the tower something was going on.
There was no howl of the wind as there previously was, no hum, no anything we knew we had to move on, so we picked up our steps and we hurried along, into a preview of sorrow with a soul of its own. The door was left open and aggie was there, with three brooding witches and a body lay bare. There were silence and candles of unholy light, with gargoyles and creatures of the ceremonious rite.

(Are you appreciating my rhythm of poetry Doctor, I go off now and then.)

There is dark arcadia in the head of Orpheus. Unsettling dreams that are not of this kind,

Through the snowy apparitions and the winds that befall us,

It is but a dream to awaken from, at some point left behind.

Sail away to the north, east, and west, and bury my bones in this old wooden chest, to a place that I know... Where the angels find rest.

From the demons that seldom relinquish their quest.

(Charlie, courtesy of the Atlas Yacht club.)

"Agatha bright and sad - she observes and accepts, Her Spirit self, the soul of Lilith, a bridge of sorrows."

(A page from Agatha Fitz Oswald's journal)

As a child, nothing is ever explained to you. The maenads did not and do not allow questions. There are so many things that you could never understand if they have to be explained to you. You have to be able to interpret the information and know that someday through realization you will understand it and not judge.

You have to work on that understanding alone by yourself. If you demand to know the answers to quickly and require an explanation you will not get one.

No one tests you no one questions you on what you have learned,. You retell it in your maturity when you have someone to pass it onto. Unknowingly I have been taught to do that, I am doing it.

Aggie XXXX__

In the Belltower one night, Aggie said there was no need for psych wards, prisons, or courts. Life itself was the teacher; there was not one person or rule. As a maenad, there is a constant awakening of responsibility. You learn that life is a reward from the Viking spirit. The doors open and you open into something you have learned. It is so simple.

A letter from John Morris our Magister Ludi. I received it in November of that year.

Charles,

I am addressing this to you but it is for Sean Anthony as well, I have no idea of his location, I am hoping that you might. After what we have been through I am wondering if we can ever have a meeting again. The Atlas yacht club has earned its wings as a legitimate club after our ordeal. With that being said, who would ever believe it? I for one am bound to never talk about it except with the surviving members of The Atlas Yacht club, through the years. I hope Sean Anthony is alright. We must try to find him, you know. I think he may be in England.

Here is the reason for my letter after all this time of silence. Although in my heart I know there should be no reason needed, I hope that we shall stay close for all our lives. You are a dear friend of mine. I can go as far as to say that, you and Sean Anthony may be the closest thing to family I have.

Being a student of comparative religion, philosophy, psychology, and related disciplines for well over twenty years, I am well aware of the profound and irreconcilable differences between different religions and beliefs.

I am not sure where I am going with this reasoning, especially in the short space of a letter. I agree that it is fascinating to study the endless variety of spiritual expression in the world. However at some point, if one wishes to be serious and make spiritual progress, one must choose a path and that means rejecting other paths. This kind of discernment is what I don't see much of in your letters.

I do not think you are criminally insane, It is ridiculous that my letters of endorsement for you were laughed out of the room. But you must remember they have never met a maenad and probably would not have lived to talk about it if they did. I can't say I blame you for burning it all down. With the disappearance of the moon cursor, the vast fortune of historical wealth uncovered in the Wunder Krammer, and of course Aggie, in her wretched state; quite a bit to answer to.

I have nightmares of what you must have gone through.

The ideas these terms hold are identical to my own beliefs that of my own beliefs to freeing from guilt or sin or deliver one from the power, consequences, or effects of sin. The term they use in your case is Justify...it is much closer to the ancient intent than the historical or the judicial. I use modern terms to make sure that the meaning they carry is clear and precise in the sense of clearing from sin.

On my behalf, I am on your side and will continue my research on your behalf in hopes that my work will find you justified, redeemed, or condemned.

I hope to visit you soon when you are allowed guest visitation of course.

As always, your Magister Ludi, John.

These messages flashed through my mind every time I try to recall any precise accuracy. They are images interrupted. Let us suppose you are watching a movie. and you keep getting up, to get a beer or some crackers or go to the bathroom, whatever the interruption and each time you return a different action sequence is happening on the screen, none related to the one you last witnessed. But still, you are aware that you are still watching the same movie.

Well, these bits of information are filtering into my mind the same way Doctor. Sometimes a distracting excerpt of poetry from Aggie, a laborious incoherent letter from the Ludi, or some distracting trivial bit of imagery before this whole mess… I am sorry Doctor Bursar if I am no help to you. I am sorry no evidence of anything exists that could substantiate my rantings. I burnt it all down to the ground. I am sure Aggie's bones are in the ashes somewhere. I know that finding them or any evidence of her would incriminate me for murder, but I assure you she was already dead, I merely cremated her so to speak, the most affordable and easiest way possible. I suppose that's grounds for madness; isn't it.

"Fitzy's body was the center of their circle. They took him away was all I could remember, he was carried by the maenads and placed on the moon cursor. When we awoke, all three of us magister Ludi, Sean Anthony, and myself, we were out on the sea with Aggie, who now was normal again and steering the boat. I looked around a little bleary. As I came to my senses I reached over to Sean Anthony who was coming to also. Ludi was rolling around about three yards away from us. What I remember most distinctly is Old Fitzy sprawled across the cold box. I was shrieking in horror at the sight of him. And why was he not wrapped in the canvas sail as we left him? Aggie was out of it, she just sailed toward the caverns. As we got closer the waves picked up, the fog came in making visibility almost zero. Needless to say, we feared for our lives. Sean Anthony had climbed to the top deck to look out… holding steadfastly to the mast to a lookout. The Ludi clutched his knapsack and held on tightly to a rail in what was as close to a fetal position as anyone could get. Water was coming in, only Aggie had complete control in a somnambulist trance. Now and then I looked out into the sea and thought I saw something silvery breaching the waves, I suspected we were being guided by the maenads. The maenads have become almost invisible against the gray fog and misty sea… only the fire in those awful eyes stood out in contrast as we dipped and rose.

I made my way to Aggie and put my hand on her shoulder; She turned facing me and snarled in a terrible grimace. She looked straight away with a stare that sent me trembling. It was then that I knew what she had on her mind. We pulled in behind the granite jetty in the little passage the route that led into to Dog's mouth, the wind picked up, it was October, The water was already Icey. Ludi accumulated some frost on his curly locks. Sean Anthony wrapped rags he had found around his hands to sustain his grip.

Ludi unraveled himself from the bench and stumbled over to an entrance door that led to a lower quarter It was then that he discovered that he would remember his whole life. Ludi while in the captain's quarters discovered a hidden room known as the wunder Krammer.

THE WUNDERKAMMER

of the heart saying
strange
strange
it's not as if such fastenings could ever contain
The regular yearning wing-beat of my evenings
Alice Oswald, from Falling awake

The cabin John Morris fell into was a blessing and a curse. It was all for respect for the dead and title, Captain Oswald Fitzoswalds quarters on the moon cursor, and much more. It was everything he was to become since its renovation. Like I said the moon cursor was not much more than a Lobster boat when Captain Fitzy discovered it at auction and fell in love with it. But now at the time of his death, it is all from benefactor to custodian of his heart-mind, and soul.

If a vessel the sort that the Moon cursor represents to the hearts and minds of the esteemed members of the Atlas Yacht Club could ever personify into something human, then the Captain's chamber of that ship was its soul. It was to be called The wunder Kramer.

They were small cabinets of glass displays of bone and ivory. Scrimshaw carvings outlined with brown script inked deep into the material they were carved upon. The peculiar range and background of these displays went from mildly spellbinding to museum-quality antiques. They were surprisingly well kept in some suspended in antiquity for hundreds of years. Besides miniature paintings and art, the more visceral pieces were in lead crystal and lead crystal containers object d' art like hair and fish. Some were whole scales of sea creatures of florescent iridescence, truly beautiful to behold.

There were wall mountings of the jawbone as some fishermen are apt to collect, shark perhaps or whale … but these were not that. These were almost human in their construction. The mandible similarities are the bone that forms the lower part of the skull, and along with the maxilla (upper jaw), forms the mouth structure. Movement of the lower jaw opens and closes the mouth and also allows for the chewing of food. The lower set of teeth in the mouth is rooted in the lower jaw.

There are other oddities as well, many were not explained until much later when John Morris Our magister Ludi was able to research much further many years later. For instance, one type of Genus he discovered was not on a wall but in a long tubular type bottle. It was a type of squid.

The vampire squid is a small (12-inch-long) cephalopod found in deep temperate and tropical seas. Originally thought to be an octopus because it lacks the two long tentacles that usually extend past a squid's eight arms, the vampire squid possesses characteristics of both squid and octopi and occupies its order in taxonomy (scientific classification).

Its huge, bright blue eyes — proportionally the largest in the animal kingdom — dark color, and the velvety, cloak-like webbing that connects its arms give the vampire squid its common name. Its scientific name, *Vampyroteuthis infernalis,* literally means "vampire squid of Hell"! While it does not suck blood like its mythical namesake, the vampire squid is a "living relic" that evolved from an ancestor of the octopus, and its lineage goes back 165 million years in the fossil record.

The vampire squid is an extremophile inhabiting the dark ocean depths from 2,000-3,000 feet. If threatened, this defensive deep-sea Dracula does not eject ink, as do most of its cephalopod cousins. Nor can it change color to confuse intruders the way its shallow-water cousins can; living as it does in the deep ocean, where little light penetrates color-changing is a pointless strategy. Instead, the vampire squid squirts a copious cloud of sticky, bioluminescent mucus toward would-be predators.

Organisms that glow make their light from chemical reactions. Fireflies have a protein called luciferase. It brings together with oxygen and a pigment called luciferin to create light. Other organisms have different ways of getting up a glow.

This glow can serve different purposes. Animals such as fireflies glow to attract mates. Others, such as the glass squid, emit light from under their eyes that makes them invisible to hungry predators below. Undersea tube worms produce mucus that glows on its own.

That slime can mark predators with a sticky blue glow for days and serve as a "burglar alarm" if the predator comes near again. And bacteria in the ocean might light up just hitch a ride. They can get swallowed by a larger animal for a free trip across the sea.

Another wall mounting was a Payara, A freshwater fish, that had horrible spiky teeth similar to a vampire, it was nicknamed the vampire fish.

Besides the sea man's instruments for navigation, there were maps so old that some of the land formations no longer existed. There were logs and journals containing drawings of ancient mariners and their battles with sea creatures. Bubbling volcanoes and underwater mines. Pirate logs and love Vanitas of all sorts and kinds.

In a drawer, there was a collection of shrunken heads, along with a map of cannibal islands. So how it was that Old Fitzy came into these Objects of curiosity? He was a neighborhood old salt; never left the waters that bound New Jersey by all accounts from Aggie.

So who owned all this? Was the captain the custodian to some other maritime museum? Is this whole epic a Gallant Ghost story?

It was becoming clearer that the moon cursor was some kind of a queen; Or possessed by the spirit of a queen. Invisible and strong, she rules the sea and the creatures therein… especially the maenads. The wunder Krammer was haunted by paintings; Dutch we believe, alongside some beautifully rendered seascapes by Ivan Konstantine Aivazovsky the Russian-Armenian Romantic painter known for his depictions of seascapes, for which he is considered one of the greatest marine artists in history. This prompted Sean Anthony to clear space by the latrine entrance and scribble in his best graffiti style the words{Sean Anthony was here} famous artist and sculptor. The moon cursor was not amused… she rocked the boat almost tipping it, sending a subtle message that any form of mockery would not be tolerated. Protocol and respect; old school discipline will be admonished.

There was one painting in particular that implied a partial understanding it was a painting of the back of a nude woman

The painting shows a woman with her back turned, with a bare torso by an oval mirror that reflects her face and the top of her chest. Her left-hand rests on a green dressing table in the image left. On the table, there is also a box with an open lid. With her right hand, she has lifted and taken to the brown hair that is tightly put up with center parting. Her big red left earlobe has a gold glistening earring. Her right earring is also seen, not in the mirror, and hairstyles are also different in the mirror. The head is turned slightly to the left and sunk.

The woman's lower body is draped with a white cloth, which is well down her buttocks. Her right leg seems to be slightly bent upward.

The woman is located offset to the left relative to the centerline of the image, whereas the mirror is on the right. The oval mirror with the wooden frame mirrors to face viewed approximately in the middle of the mirror. The mirror has a size so that only the top portion of the woman's breasts is seen. The woman raised her right arm that covers parts of the mirror image so viewers cannot see the bottom part of the face. In the mirror image is also seen that women do not consider themselves in the mirror, but the gaze is directed downward to the left; there is no eye contact with the viewer.

The wall where the mirror hangs is plain, however, with some text. On the left of the picture is an oblique shadow on the wall and down the left wall. On the bottom right is a panel at the height of her thighs. In the reflection, one can see a closed door. It was Dutch; we are supposing John was not able to find out much about it.

Aggie was still operating on Automatic pilot and did not share our enthusiasm over this.

The Ludi came across a jewelry box. Black enamel was the best he could describe it. It had soapstone figures attached to it along the sides and top. It was Oriental from the day. Mandarin if Ludi's research is accurate and it most likely always is. The inside was lined with silk. Ink images were places all over with no set design, random skulls, and death symbols. Boney hands that of a grim reaper perhaps. There were four tiny compartments each one had a ring

They were elaborating each one different very beautiful, demonstrating elegance and grace. It was not thought to represent the macabre and sinister function to which it was intended for.

Lucretia Borgia immortalized poisoning in fourteen hundred however, except for some Gothic minded fashionistas the poison ring itself has fallen somewhat out of practical use in these modern times, Forensic technology has come a long way. But here is what the Magister Ludi has to say about it.

From some notes, I kept a record of from John Morris. (Magister Ludi);

Ancient Romans sometimes used poison rings to commit suicide when a painful death was unavoidable. The historian Pliny, the Elder (23-79 CE) recounts how a Roman government official escaped torture by taking a bite out of his poison ring (a thin shell was the container for the poison). The teenaged Emperor Heliogabalus (203 CE – 222 CE), feared because of his cruelty and notorious for his debauchery, wore a poison ring – but was assassinated before he could ingest its contents.

A poison ring may have also played a part in ending an aristocratic feud between two powerful families in the middle Ages. In the 21st century, archeologists in Bulgaria unearthed a bronze ring with a secret compartment. It is theorized that poison in the ring may have been used by Dobrotitsa (1347-1386), the ruler of Despotate of Dobrudja, against an influential family in the Kaliakra fortress.

The appeal of poison rings (or secret rings) transcends centuries.

Poison rings – alternately referred to as pillbox, compartment, locket, or vessel rings – also had a benign purpose. During the Middle Ages, they were often used to hide relics of saints, like bits of their hair, bone, and teeth, which were thought to protect the wearer from various calamities and maladies. During the Renaissance, the aristocracy used them to hold cologne, locks of hair, and portraits of loved ones. This one however that we have stumbled upon had a secret compartment disguised under a false bottom that still had the poisons intact.

It will be interesting to see what Aggie has to say about any of this if we ever come out of this alive. We never got the chance...

The Caverns are ahead. In this miserable darkness, we were all convinced we were surely going to die, if not for maenads and most certainly some darker forces we were led over the pounding waves and jagged rocks that most certainly were meant for the demise of anyone who dared come this close to the caverns. I feared to look overboard; I did not want to look into the blazing eyes of those creatures. I could feel with the natural intuition vested in all of us that they wanted to feast on my blood, but something more powerful had reigned over them.

What did it look like I wonder; the embodiment of the moon cursor. Was she that enchanting nude in the painting? Had she one time had a lover? Is she such a restless queen that she seeks revenge in humanity forevermore? Old Captain Fitzy, custodian to the renovated lobster boat, possessed by a vampire queen.

Is it AMPHITRITE? the goddess-queen of the sea, wife of Poseidon, and eldest of the fifty Nereides? She was the female personification of the sea--the loud-moaning mother of fish, seals, and dolphins, Or was she a lover of Bacchus and courtesan to the harem of maenads that entertained the Gods. What, overthrew them in their raging glory, I can't help but wonder... what upset the natural order of things in their ancient world? What is the vampires' lust for blood in the sea world except that they are mammals and not fish? Perhaps they choose the sea to hide more easily from humans.

The shape change is true. However, they cannot stay out of water for very long or they age dramatically. But in the water, they must come up for air periodically like a whale or a dolphin. Those teeth, the ones mounted on the wunder Krammer wall they are maenads. I would bet anything on it.

It comes to me now while I am in and out of clarity partly due to my medication here at the dunes and partly because the human side of me will not allow me to remember as the evil side will not allow me to forget.

What saved us that night? What, who- brought us back safe? I don't know, but let me continue with my confession of how we disposed of Fitzy's body.

I am here Doctor, are you writing this down? When I go the story goes. The Ludi will not help you, and Sean Anthony is missing in exile, parts unknown… maybe never to be heard from again. The Atlas Yacht club has been reduced to a pile of rubble and buried mermaid tears.

And Aggie, oh, she is gone. I watched her clothes burn dry and brittle. I did not know the flames would reach the tower so quickly, I tried to save her. I rolled her across the floor but all was lost. She was too comatose to understand what was going on. Her hair began to burn. The more flammable objects around the room began to go up. I had doused the gasoline outside but not on the Belltower thinking I would have time to grab her and scuttle her out to safety. I wanted to save Aggie, I just did not know what I was to witness when I found her. I ran to the steps everything behind me was engulfed in flames, I looked out a passing window I felt relief. I thought for a moment I saw Fitzy on top of the moon cursor covered with flames waving his arms like a madman. I did not he was long gone the moon cursor had returned to the sea. I watched and I could not believe my eyes. Completely inflamed the Mooncurssor was sailing up the canal, a ball of flames. it was headed toward the caverns. I watched it in awe. The heat was against my back. The maenads had it. They were bringing their queen home.

To finish what happened, I never told you how we completed our funeral arrangements for Fitzy.

The Moon cursor crashed on to some jetty rocks and locked in place. All of us stood silent. We were wet to the bone with mist and splashing waves.

Something passed from the boat, It shivered, the hull of the boat shivered, like a dog shaking off water after a bath..something crawled across the jetty stones and slithered into the caverns. Seconds later two maenads came forth seemingly from nowhere and boarded the moon cursor. One came forward and outstretched it hand holding dominion over us. While the other wen to the cold box where old Fitzy was clumsily stuffed into. The maenad kneeled beside him touching his head. He began to rise slowly. He was completely ripped open his eyes plucked out from the crows. He stood feebly his seas legs wobbling. He began to move his feet one before the other until he was at the stern of the boat and then whisked away in a murky rush. The maenad attending us was gone Aggie was asleep on the floor. I saw them all, Sean Anthony, the Ludi, and myself I thought they were all dead, but they were sleeping. It was then I felt the ship move. A shiver came over the boat. I fell to the deck, When I awoke we were ashore. The moon cursor was docked the same as it ever was. We were cast off…our welcome had expired.

I took Aggie into my arms, as she began to awaken; I squeezed her and kissed her lips, never before had she been so attractive to me. The salty brine on her skin was exquisite. I smelled blood as she smelled blood. Everything was different. The color of the sea. The look in one's eyes.

As aggie awoke I was still holding her. She smiled of all things as though disturbed from a magical dream. I could not speak, I did not have to.

"What happened'? I asked.

"The most wonderful thing". She said.

"That you could see me as I see you". she said.

"I had a wish, granted Charlie."

I have been hexed?" I asked.

No, only when you see me, you will see me as I see you, That is what I wished for. That you can taste me as a maenad, you can smell the blood, for those moments. You could lust as we lust. I looked into her eyes and saw them as they were. Circular waves of opal fire beautiful like her mothers. captivating and intense. I could not look away. For the first time, I saw Aggie completely. It was amazing. I was in love for the first time in my life.

I heard a moan from behind me. It was the Magister Ludi awakening from a deep sleep, rolling around on the beach like a large land mammal. With reluctance, I separated myself from Aggie to help John. We looked for Sean Anthony but found no trace anywhere. We feared he never made it back. John stood up and saw something in the road, it was Sean Anthony's backpack, He had stumbled away and gone probably half insane. We feared that he went into town and was discovered in his wild state of mind. We did not need any attention coming down on us not now. I knew everything would be alright. Sean would know what to do.

It is his unconventional lifestyle that would help us all now. I must find a time and place to record this into the annals of The Atlas Yacht club.

The Magister Ludi sat erect on the sand and gathered his senses. After shaking his head in a revelation he quickly arose and stormed the Moon cursor...

The wunder Krammer he cried... those things I must get them, the books, all the secrets the lives the history are all in that wunder Krammer...

The Ludi pulled the ramp to the boat and climbed up haphazardly. The bulk of his body and the pull of his clothes tugging at him made him out to be a comic spectacle. Because I was with Aggie I am experiencing my new maenad senses. And the futility of Ludi's seems ludicrous.

When he got to the deck he ran to the Captain's quarters, there was a lock on it. Frustrated, he found a crowbar and began ripping at the door. When he finally burst in, nothing could have prepared him for it. There literally was nothing. No wunder Krammer no anything. He tore through the walls for secret compartments... nothing, just broken veneer. Aside from some items that were Fitzy's, nothing on the scale of a wunderkammer.

The Ludi came to the deck and pulled up a chair he sat on it nesting his head in his hands he began to speak.;

"Ole worm": He said.

"I was Ole worm for a day."

"We don't understand John what is it?"

In the tradition of the Atlas yacht club, john went on to tell us all about Ole worm with tears in his eyes. He pulled once again from his dubious messenger bag, a book of collectors and bizarre collections.

As usual, we braced ourselves for a coming omen. Everything is connected in this God-forsaken town.

Born in 1588, Ole Worm — also known as Ole Wurm or Olaus Wormius — was a Danish savant who became a professor of Latin, Greek, medicine, and physics. He was born in the Danish city of

Aarhus, where his father was mayor. Growing up, he enjoyed an exceptional education, first attending grammar school in Aarhus, and later traveling to Germany, Italy, France, England, Belgium, Luxembourg, and the Netherlands. He studied under the famous taxonomist Caspar Bauhin, visited the famous cabinet of Ferrante Imperato, and modeled himself after the famous Aldrovandi. In 1611, Worm earned his doctorate in medicine, after compiling a dissertation on just about every disease known at the time.

While on his European grand tour, he started collecting unusual objects. Worm's interests covered natural objects, human artifacts, mythical creatures, and ancient inscriptions. After his grand tour concluded, he began working at the University of Copenhagen, eventually becoming a professor of medicine in 1624. Meanwhile, he built one of the most well-known curiosity cabinets in Europe, and in 1655 posthumously published *Museum Wormianum*, or *History of the Rarer Things both Natural and Artificial, Domestic and Exotic, which the author collected in his house in Copenhagen*. As the title suggests, the catalog included natural objects (minerals, plants, and animals), and human-made objects. Collection catalogs were a new kind of publication in the mid-17th century, and *Museum Wormianum* counted among the earliest examples.

From Ole Worm's Cabinet of Wonder: Natural Specimens and Wondrous Monsters at the Biodiversity Heritage Library

Worm passed along remarkable stories if he believed they came from reliable sources, describing the wondrous attributes of bezoar stones grown inside animal bodies, for instance. Yet he also advocated investigations of unusual objects where possible. Not surprisingly, he considered the authority of ancient "experts" a hindrance to clear thinking. The worm was among the first to establish that the fabled unicorn horn and actual narwhal tusks were the same, as he explained in a paper he delivered in 1638. (His motivation might not have been entirely altruistic; his in-laws were in the business of prescribing the seemingly superior narwhal tusk to treat a host of maladies.) He also disproved the spontaneous generation of lemmings (thought to fall from the sky, perhaps), though he didn't doubt the spontaneous generation of some other organisms.

Beyond his contributions to natural history, Worm laid the foundations of modern archaeological surveys, recommending an assiduous collection of information from every archaeological site. Some historians have argued that Worm's collection might have spurred the interest of the young Niels Stensen (Steno), who in turn laid the foundations for modern geology. Steno grew up just a few streets away from Worm's curiosity cabinet. Unfortunately, Worm's collection did not outlast him very long. His small museum was shuttered after his death, the specimens sent to other collections. Some of the objects likely landed in the Royal Danish Kunstkammer, which Steno did visit, probably more than once.

It all goes back to the Danes in someway Aggie... you are a Viking girl

In high school they thought I was a pirate girl, when can I just be a regular girl like everybody else.

"Not anytime soon. Aggie,"

"The maenads won't let you go."

I looked up at John for the first time since his story.

Poor, cold, undetached, fact eating John.

He doesn't realize how his cold, straight, unfiltered logic, is breaking my heart.

Before I go on let me tell you this.…

It is about Sean Anthony. As I said he has fled on our return we do not know where. Also as I have mentioned, Aggie John and myself were washed up on the shore, exhausted, and partly drowned. We thought Sean Anthony had not returned or was drowned during the mayhem, I recovered his backpack about fifty yards down the road off Constable Hook. Until this day, John and I have only gotten partial rambling letters from different parts of the world regarding his well-being and whereabouts. From the form and incoherent ramblings of his letters, he might be somewhat functionally insane.

SEAN ANTHONY

D arrived at Earls Court in October on X-X He contracted a mild fever and was taken to a medical clinic by some friends that were expecting him and he was granted the luxury to stay with. Richard Blair and recent girlfriend Renee Frost received him at the station two-thirty in the afternoon. The flight from JFK airport to be close to five hours, Sean Anthony arrived with a little more than a passport some travel money he had saved, and a suitcase. His backpack with all or most of his valuables was lost somewhere.

The interns at the Medical clinic were friendly and suspicious of their American patients. The down and out scrounge riff-raff of all sorts, from the lower quarters of Earls, was always being dragged in at ungodly hours but this was peculiar and a bit more interesting.

Not your usual drug addict, domestic abuse casualty, or drunkard this character was an American who just arrived, was unkempt and disheveled, wild-eyed, and completely paranoid. The usual battery of interrogation went smoothly and there was no reason to suspect him of any foul play; an expatriate perhaps roaming the globe seeking refuge in the arms of any nefarious rebel group that might have him. Having cleared all hurdles and resting for two days he returned to Earl's court with Richard and things began to get normal.

Within a week they began working on some projects together and he was helping earn his keep, this would ensure him some time to stay, until he could get it together enough to land him a squatter flat on the other side of town, restoring a measure of privacy to his friend's life. The squatters flat would allow him more space to paint and pursue some business opportunities with galleries he had worked under in the past. All paperwork in the order he starts fresh away from Constable Hook and the Horror. Perhaps one day he might even accept it as just a bad dream and never have to fear it again; hardly unlikely.

Richard and Rene were entertaining guests one evening And Sean Anthony was there. Paula and Michael, friends of the host came on time and brought with them an added guest one Leonia Poutine. A friend of Rene's from art school was staying in London. Coincidently with Leonia being a third wheel and Sean Anthony the renegade unchaperoned guest, the idea was that everyone could pair off nicely and a pleasant evening could be had by all.

Leonia was a talented woman, bright and resourceful; she was twenty-six with the face of an angel. Her eyes were dazzling blue. Clear like pristine ocean water, cerulean, at times almost silver, like the lining said to be found in clouds.

Sean Anthony sensed it the second he looked at her. He scanned her from the doorway as a ripple of sensation passed through his body.

It has been a while since he was normal in that way. The Atlas Yacht club had castrated him from his normal desires. He felt he was being punished for some evil. However, the judge and jury were not of a heavenly spiritual world; but of one down under, beneath the sea. They held court in a watery cavern somewhere across the ocean. A place where the earth breathes death and the smell of the rancid flesh is your own.

Sean Anthony cleaned up nicely: showered, shaved, and even was mindful to remove bits of paint from around his cuticles and fingernails. He was able to shop some rumble sales and discount markets through-out London and white chapel finding decent clothes and accessories.

Over those last few weeks, an amazing recovery transpired. However, to spite outward appearances when he looked in a mirror he was careful not to look too closely, becoming aware of some involuntary twists and tics in his countenance, pre-mature aging signs inflicted on him by the horror. If he looked too closely into his own eyes, the murky tides of Key Harbor began to swirl about, his irises at times becoming a whirlpool of sludge and mire. His light brown eyes, gifted to see the world in all its primitive and artistic nuances, have become a mood board for the memories collected from the moon cursor.

This is an episode worth noting; an excerpt from a letter I received from him about that evening.

We were comparing notes for a time, we three, never meeting again at the Old spye inn. The Atlas Yacht club; went online so to speak in the form of handwritten letters. This was before the time I took it upon myself to burn all of it to the ground... Poor Aggie, when I saw her there.

This is how Sean Anthony framed the meeting.

I am paraphrasing.

"All went well to a point. There were music and food, I even helped prepare some dishes, my bohemian hobo recipes were not encouraged so I prepared traditional steak fries with cheese and presented them as hors de oeuvres. I have to admit it reminded me of home... Home? What does that mean to us? I know we never talk about it. You had mentioned in joking of burning down the house. You said it could never be for anyone else; the Atlas yacht club I mean. Do you still feel that way?"

Later he went on to say about the party;

Oh, Leonia was great, Charming as hell. What could I say about perfection? She wore this really cute cocktail dress, with this Japanese print design. Sweet. She seemed to like me so we talked and everything seemed to veer nicely into common ground. You would have liked her Charlie, She reminded me, Aggie, a little only without the demons and the meanads... Oh, I have normalized it now. It is Okay, they are natural. I am one with it; if I might be so transcendental. She was amazing Charlie, she was. Like in the movies, like in a foreign film or something right. But, like in all those movies... there should be a tragedy right, I mean something outside paradise that fucks up your shit. Well, this was it, Charlie.

It was evening, we were on a small terrace that overlooked this nice English terrace. There was like fountains and shit, just like in the movies. You know like we always talk about. I felt like I was sixteen years old Charlie, you know like we always talk about, that kind of romance feeling you want to enact with a girl. Well, it happened, at least this time anyway. But then something else happened. And this is what I am writing to you about.

I looked into her eyes, Charlie. They were these beautiful eyes. Two orbs of China blue that was so reflective of the light that they never seemed to focus on anything... I mean you could not tell if she was looking at you or through you, over your head or behind you. It was amazing the dreaminess of it -and all, you know Charlie? You know what I am saying right?

And then it happened Charlie, little specks of gold began to circulate her pupils, they caused trails. Her eyes got big Charlie, like bulbous or, something like that. I was afraid Charlie, I was afraid, they just kept swirling. I didn't feel weird or anything I just felt like it was happening. All very natural. She wanted to be kissed Charlie, she wanted to be kissed, and I wanted to oblige, but I was afraid... afraid I would bite her lips. I wanted to taste her blood, Charlie. She was enticing me to taste her blood.

Do you remember when we washed ashore at constable hook; that morning after the horror. I was already gone by the time you guys regained consciousness. One of those things had at me, but it wasn't a creature it made itself half-human looking like a mermaid, it was calling me Like Leonia was calling me that night. Tempting me... It wanted to be kissed, kissed by a human... but it did not know how to kiss and it ripped at my lip the teeth brushed across me biting into me several times. I think I was infected with something. Because I wanted to rip into Leonia that night, not for sex or kisses, I wanted to taste her blood. The passion was there to get at her liver. I see it now; I see it more frequently; The swirling in their eyes. I smell the blood Charlie like perfume. That thing raped me Charlie it allowed my getaway. It did not rip me open. I had to go I cannot tell you any more about myself. I am on the move again. That is all I can say.

Remember me in your memories, I will be writing the Ludi also you guys can have a story to tell at the Atlas yacht club that is for sure.

Your brother in arms.

Sean Anthony.

Compiled from some partial notes and letters I have received from whatever sources available to me at the time. The scant remains of his belongings and some artwork were burned at Constable Hook when I went berserk.

Doctor Bursar rolls his eyes, but carefully took notes. Do-dah do-dah. There is something I don't trust in this Dr. Burser cat…like he is acting.

He makes a face with dull surprise
All the livelong day.
Nurses feed me Meds,
Someone makes my bed
My home is called the Dunes for Loons
That is where I rest my head.

Do you see how I did that? I just made that up off the cuff. "How are you? I'm fine."

So whatever happened to Aggie, in all those in-between years before I went back for that final visit? It could not have been good. I still torture myself over the cowardly way I left after Fitzy's death. How could I have taken part in that sordid affair, bringing a man's dead body to a formation of rocks in the middle of a harbor in the dark of night and leaving him in the hands of those serpentine creatures with no remorse or thought for a decent burial?

Because it was the only thing to do, that's why. Aggie had complete control over it a myrmidon, she faithfully followed protocol… Those old books and enchiridion that were being knocked around that day, when I encountered the maenads for the first time.

That poem,

"Like an old whore forgotten whose teeth went all rotten and her hair was the color of wet wood and whiskey." It was the moon cursor all along.

My transpicuous observations move forward…

"On the floor lies a sonnet with the perfume still on it; stained with tears from a hundred old sailors and me."

Of course, old Fitzy, one of the many casualties left in the wake of the moon cursor.\

The ole' Lady Moon cursor has been possessing ships for centuries… her first love might have been a Berserk Viking or maybe before she might have driven Ulysses mad.

"The first to come forth was an oblique and grease smeared whore. Whose savage nails and crinkly hair dripped fragrant musk. Like a maenad maiden above the ascetic's reverent hand."

"What shall we carve on this beloved ivory face?

Some scrimshaw designs on whalebone back at the mysterious wunder Krammer… gone without a trace. I told you the boat burned I soaked it myself with gasoline. It was going back to the caverns… I saw it from a distance a fiery ball slamming against the rocks, purple smoke, and steam sizzling busting up on the granite jetty. The sounds, of mosquitoes bobbing and weaving in and out of the smoke curls.

To gleam on a girl's raven hair within the abyss."

Insects and flying fowl of the air he rushed to wedge his chest against that foe. The sea that strove to crush them. The dreams all night long that pursued of huge wings and claws, Opened to the daybreak of half-opened eyes. The dawn smiled, But still, the dreams poured from my brain like swirling mist.

From a book of no title; notes I copied from Aggie's journal.

-Swirling mist like those eyes. The eyes Sean Anthony is haunted by.

The last words I heard from Sean Anthony were this.

January/

Charlie, I have signed on to a merchant's vessel for steady work, many of the recruits here are desperate men. Some are escaping the law; some have terrible pasts they must escape from. The work is will be sometimes hard, all the better, it will keep me from my thoughts. The dangers of being out to sea do not frighten me, I feel I am doomed at any rate. I do not want to return to the mainland living. It is best to be around these friends for I am one of them. Much worse I fear. I know that somewhere out here on the open seas deep where the secrets sleep I will see something silver beneath the crest of each wave. Those eyes will greet me. My vampiress, soulmate will protect me.

I was looking over the manual they gave us as part of the maritime training required for service. There is a prayer we are required to learn for spiritual strength during dangerous times. Get this:

"Blessed be the grace of god our one eternal father!

It is he from his grace and love created fish and sea. It is he who brims our nets and fills our hearts with joy: Oh comrades raise your hand on high and cry," Our Father"!

I dare not. Not now.

Each time I see the fish scales flash with silver, the net dropped with foam; the googling eyes of fish strung by earthen fishermen, I cannot turn off my thoughts of Captain Fitzy standing in the doorway of the moon cursor protecting his lady. And when he died she moved on- taking the ghosts with her, the most unfortunate casualties that have left human blood sweat, and tears on the deck of that ship.

"I am scared I am going to spend the rest of my life Lusting blood, no matter where I am or where I go." The spirits indeed have come to my brother to walk the earth but carry no flame in their heart.

on Sean Anthony. Collected letters fragments of conversation.

I fuss with these old notebooks, journals, and pagers from Aggie, I suppose you can say they are love letters, some of them anyway. I took a break today and walked around the grounds. I saw my friend Lenny one of the fantastic anomalies I compare myself to around here.

He is a lifer.; brought in as a young man, Lenny kidnapped a high school glee club sweetheart and held her in the custodial basement of an abandoned factory for three days for forcing her to sing "Low how my rose is blooming" at the top of her lungs. A passer-by heard the troubled tear strained voice echoing from the abandoned parking lot and called the police. The girl was unharmed; Lenny was sitting on a milk crate conducting an invisible choir of angels, peacefully absorbed in a cloud of sublime schizophrenia; Oblivious to the chaos taking place around him, he left peacefully. Looking back over his shoulder at the visibly distraught diva, He whispered, "Encore" as two burly officers hauled him away.

Lenny wanted to be a poet, what secured his internment at the Dunes for Loons somewhat permanently was an unfortunate incident he had no control over. The story goes like this.

He was in the lounge of the west wing campus; non-violent patience can go to the west wing and hangout. He was writing one day at his desk minding his beeswax when Oscar till, a fellow inmate, visiting while on experimental parole, for no reason at all stabbed him in the head with a ballpoint pen. The metal tip lodged into his brain. It was not fatal and was tended to rather unceremoniously. However, the intrusion did pass through his skull piercing the part of his brain that produces dreams.

Lenny began having hallucinations that he was meeting and conversing with dead poets that would tell him secrets about their lives. He began believing it.

Then, one day he wrote this astonishingly beautiful poem about a magical place one of his imaginary poets told him about.

The doctors assigned to his case are still baffled by how Lenny could have done this, being his poetry had always been very bland and not like poetry at all, according to one doctor. But still, Lenny waxed on with great detail about the life and times of his poet friend.

I sometimes think That Doctor Bursar suspects that I am the same kind of bug. Except, I am not mad. (to quote Dali)…now I fully relate, yes I fully relate.

Here is a Note I kept from Aggie. Poor, sweet Aggie.

April XX

"I'm a mess of conflicting impulses—I'm self-determining and simple-minded at times and I also want to belong and share and be a part of the complete circle. I doubt that I'm the only one who feels this way. It's the core of monster making. Wanna' make a monster? Take the parts of yourself that make you uncomfortable—your weaknesses, bad thoughts, vanities, and fits of hunger—write them down then roll them up into a big round paper ball and eat them. It's too ugly to be human. It's too ugly to be a maenad. Children are afraid of the dark because they have nothing real to work with. Adults are afraid of themselves. Oh, we're a mess, we maenads, with our silver flesh—crossbreeds of humans and sea creatures, with paper balls of handwritten acknowledgments stuffed inside them. Let me tell you what I do know: I am more than one thing and not all of those things are good. The truth is complicated. It's two-toned, ice cream cone on the boardwalk at Atlantic City, bittersweet. I used to think that if I told the truth I could discover something bright and shiny, I'd know it was something self-evident. Now I'm trying to lie a little more each day.

Or this one…

"When can we meet?" he began to ask and there was a part of me that wanted to meet with him very badly, and there was a part of me that was so afraid that I would push it off until later, not sure when I would be ready. Charlie was patient with me and he took his time gaining my trust until one day, I finally gave in and agreed to meet him.

THE MYSTERY OF THE MOON CURSOR

I have pinned up in my room clippings and newsprint articles about some things I have been collecting. My not so spacious cubical, municipal-run room here at the Dunes, is becoming more of a wunder Krammer of fact and fiction than just a place for me to live out my years. Not unlike a great many other mysteries that fester on Constable Hook, Key Harbor, the history of the Moon cursor has never been explained.

I also was allowed to save the things I have collected from Aggie over the years; some scrimshaw carvings on whalebone, and a few jaw bone and mandibles of shark that Fitzy had preserved.

I was with him one afternoon, early on in my innocent relationship, and witnessed first-hand how he rendered the bones.

He did explain the taxidermist procedure step by step as it was taught to him. Industry secrets passed down from old salt to old salt; the seaman's answer to relinquishing the boredom of being at sea for weeks on end.

The head of the shark was first removed and salted completely, a thick coating of coarse salt. It was then hung to dry out in the sun allowing for the skin, cartilages, and eyes along with any other soft tissue and moisture to naturally rot off. Then the skeletal bones and teeth were bleached with a peroxide solution until bone white as we know it, then at last they were carefully mounted on a scrap piece of pine or maple wood, ready for hanging. Incidentally, this same technique works just as well on maenad's head, those I have seen with my own eyes, but have none for my collection. I call them souvenirs. Mementos from a time I had vacationing at constable Hook.

One of the more memorable luxuries for tourists who come in from the cities and suburbs is to visit souvenir shops. Most people want a trinket or memorabilia of some talisman to bring home with them as a token of memory that recaps their fine experience while vacationing; a coffee cup or a sweatshirt with Cape so and so or seaside whatever… a humble memento to casual life experience.

The more Nautical motifs, however, we have come to romanticize, many having their folklore histories related to dark and not so Pollyanna beginnings can be traced back to the old sea salt. He is sometimes depicted as a saintly old man wearing a weathered sou'wester folded up at one end, boots to the knees, and a pious beard, patiently building a schooner from matchsticks or placing an old ghost ship replica into an empty rum bottle out of sheer boredom. One imagines a case or two of salted beef and a seaman's wooden chest at his bunk. In this town, his effigy has replaced the lawn jockey as the focal point to second home gardens.

No one thinks of him half-drunk fighting the quiet unadventurous hours of rest time when there is simply nothing to do except silently losing your mind at sea. Memento mori

Something has kept me alive this far as well as the other members of the Atlas yacht club. Something or someone may want me to tell this story; or, I might just be a living artifact wunder Krammer adornment for the powers that be. I have come to think of Olde Fitzy as Dracula's Renfield that way; the immortalized strong-armed, sea wise apprentice that serves the Moon cursor.

Once again, the story returns to Aggie and an arrangement in gray. The quintessential portrait of a woman accepting the hand she was dealt from the comfort of her chair; embracing the romances of a lone Belltower.

She watches the caverns. The sentinal gray lady who waits at the widow's peak for the vessels return. I have contemplated the "arrangement in gray", this way.

If the sea hag calls to mind any Victorian visual references of James McNeill whistler's mother perched in colonial dress and bonnet then your frame of reference is altogether superb and you have an old soul. With all respect to Whistler's mother, who I am sure was a fine

Lady, sitting peacefully at her seaside abode, our Aggie was nothing like that the last time I saw her.

She was so hideous and monstrously appalling I was not only inspired to burn the whole harbor down to the ground I felt it my doleful obligation to do so. Not on a whim of schizophrenic episode as they say, but as my duty; an act of love as a gentleman to my one and only Aggie.

She never had a chance folks, believe me, she never had a chance; her mother was a bloodsucking freak, and her father was an ignorant fisherman that never confessed his sins.

They are in hell somewhere, but hell might be here in this very dimension; not in Dante's cantos or Hades of the Norse Gods, but right here, in the pine skeleton frame and brick of this bell tower. The caverns are fiery brimstone that steam when the oceanic holy water washes over them.

It makes sense that there are multiple stories about ships lost at sea, or simply one's crew stumbling upon an empty ship drifting without aim and with no one aboard. This is known as a ghost ship. A ghost ship is a ship with no living crew aboard, found adrift, with its crew dead or missing without reason.

Here, in this case, the Moon cursor floating back to the caverns on fire, no one navigating it tugged by the maenads. I watched with the flames looming behind me… and Aggie burning away, so dry she went up like paper. The horror was waiting for me to return. The whole of Constable Hook needed to be purged by way of fire and water.

Even today with all of the technological advancements available, there are still some mysterious disappearances that nobody can explain. Why would the spirit of a queen maenad marry an illiterate fisherman; possess a fishing boat, do the interior decoration in late century Wunder Krammer and provoke me to burn a ghost town to the ground and then sit in an institution for the criminally insane, removing any clue to back my story.

Renfield My brother, do you still feel the pain of being misunderstood. An insane man kept in an institution. Was I not The Moon cursor faithful student as Fitzy was? Did I fail as Renfield has failed?

The entire Atlas Yacht club has dissipated, and where could they have gone?

It was that night reckoning that broke them. It was Fitzy's death and entombment, that put them over the edge that night. What is a ghost ship after all; a myth, a manifestation of the mind? The crisis of subjectivity is in the haunting. The artifact that beckons us here is the tower.

The tower according to Dr. Bursar is a phallic symbol of narcissism and sterility. I however have witnessed with my own eyes how it nothing short of a tower of Babble for demonic, shape-changing overpaid mermaids. One would not want to deny that a tower offers a position of heroic stance. Yet it was not until Aggie was sent off to live alone in her makeshift private room where she could exist for herself alone. Contemplating in isolation, receiving the spiritual gifts bestowed on her from that Godforsaken kingdom by the sea.

"Whether in the traditional religious question which mythological women like Beatrice, serves as the means of the ascent to God; or in the secular variant she serves as a creative muse Aggie was somehow left behind as the hero reaching for God as a self-sufficient creator in the form of the moon cursor another phallic vessel or the caverns a form of mount Olympia as a refuge or secret garden of unearthly delights.

Notes.
Dr. Emanuel bursar. (on my evaluation) November. XX

Having heard such codswallop over the years has reinforced in me, Charles Conliffe being of no so sound in mind and body(as they say), that torching the entire section of Constable Hook to the ground was indeed an act of mercy. When I am subjected to hear this poppycock from Bursar and his colleagues I secretly wish that a kidnap committee of two or three of those large mosquitoes would bust into one of our meetings and carry him away.

Who would believe me when I explained how he disappeared?

The final irony, however, is perhaps provided by the perspective of the young woman imprisoned within the tower. Pynchon's Oedipa Maas, despite her increasing sense of entrapment, refuses the confines of the masculine vision and presents the possibility that the very notion of the tower as a self-contained structure is an illusion. If escape I thereby rendered, so is the structure of the quest.

Such a captive maiden, having plenty of time to think, soon realizes that her tower, its height, and architecture, are like her ego only incidental: and what keeps her is magic, anonymous and malignant, visited on her from outside and for no reason at all.

Thomas Pynchon, *The crying of Lot 49*

The moon cursor it is safe to say was a Ghostship, more of a lobster boat, But, what's a girl to do, It was Fitzy's boat and Margaret queen of the maenads did her best. You can't make a silk purse from a sow's ear "as the Victorian ladies used to say. And with that Margaret and Oswald Fitz Oswald fell in love Producing one lovely daughter that I had the privilege to see off from this world in engulfment of flames.

Ghost ships of all types have been found, from old and rusty to ones in perfectly good shape, the ghost stories of these ships are completely unexplained. An unpredictable event such as an audacious storm or perhaps pirates raiding for loot may have left the ship empty inside. Many crews resort to a lifeboat when abandoning ship, and can be lost at sea or eaten up by the swelling waves of a storm. Many crews have mysteriously disappeared with no explanation.

The history of the moon cursor is ancient, she has been taking many forms since time unknown. She was there with the Greeks and Troy. She took prisoners on the hulk ships. There is the story of the Kilroy A notorious cruel prison ship, left floating off the English Channel by the north sea on its way to France; A newspaper Archive from Britain's arms reported: The prison Hulk Kilroy lost since May,17xx was reported found at the entrance to the north sea. "Everyone aboard was gruesomely slaughtered, one hundred and twenty-five prisoners and crew ripped open and not any blood to be found spilled.' according to Captain Stewart Browne.

The prisoners were a mix of soldiers, sailors, and rebellious civilians. Many were crew members from privateers—privately owned ships authorized by the Continental Congress, which had a little navy of its own, to harass and seize British vessels. To crew the privateers, their captains often relied on young men and teenagers from New England and elsewhere in the colonies. They typically had a little sailing experience but were eager for more excitement than they'd find behind a plow.

When the British captured a privateer, members of its crew were frequently offered a choice: Sign on with a British vessel or take your chances on a prison ship.

Most of the young Americans knew what imprisonment would mean. Colonial newspapers had reported on the horrific conditions and brutal treatment aboard the prison ships from the beginning, historian, Even so, the great majority of the captured sailors who had any choice in the matter took prison over serving the British. An estimated eight percent of the Americans went over to the other side, although some researchers put the number slightly higher.

Once aboard the prison ships, the recruiting efforts continued. Some prisoners were offered cash; others told that their families would starve in the streets. The horrors of the prison ships also served as a recruiting tool, making any alternative—even betraying one's country—seem attractive by comparison. Uriah Sumter, a one-time prisoner on such Hulks, marveled that, "Many were starved to death in hope of making them enroll themselves in the British Army."

A FLOATING HODGEPODGE
OF HUMAN DESOLATION

Just how bad were the conditions on these ships? The survivors' first-person accounts more than speak for themselves.

"I now found myself in a loathsome prison, among a collection of the most wretched and disgusting looking objects that I ever beheld in human form," wrote James Christen., who'd been captured as a teenage cabin steward aboard a privateer. "Here was a motley crew, covered with rags and filth; visages pallid with a disease, emaciated with hunger and anxiety, and retaining hardly a trace of their original appearance."

"I soon found that every spark of humanity had fled the breasts of the British officers who had charge of that floating receptacle of human misery; and that nothing but abuse and insult was to be expected," wrote Alexander Coffin Jr., who, as an 18-year-old sailor, was imprisoned. "But to cap the climax of infamy we were fed (if fed it might be called) with provisions not fit for any human being to make use of—putrid beef and pork, and worm-eaten bread…"

"There were continual noises during the night," wrote Fredrick Schenck, a captured master's mate from a privateer, age 25. "The groans of the sick and the dying; the curses poured out by the weary and exhausted upon our inhuman keepers; the restlessness caused by the suffocating heat and the confined and poisoned air; mingled with the wild and incoherent ravings of delirium."

Under such conditions, disease flourished. "Small-pox, dysentery, yellow fever and other contagions ran rampant in the crowded holds," notes Ronald Edgar Holmes. Although the British stationed hospital ships nearby, they were poorly supplied and soon overwhelmed with patients. As a result, many of the sick were left aboard the prison ships, where they infected others. By one estimate, at least seven prisoners died every day, and sometimes twice that number.

Many of the dead were buried on the nearby beaches, in graves so shallow that their corpses soon poked up through the sand. Prisoners aboard the ship could see the bones of their former comrades bleaching in the sun, and skulls and other remnants would turn up for many years thereafter.

One of my last letters from the Ludi was sent to me here at the Dunes.

April, xx

Charles,

In keeping with good faith, I hope this letter finds you well. For self-evident reasons, I cannot reveal my location. But I have found some articles that may interest you concerning Key Harbor, There was a purloined journal by one, Captain Horatio Polk. He manned a Trade ship that was set course for Boston from the East Indies but made entry into Key Harbor for Key Harbor, no ledger as to why. He never made entry to the port. The ship was a legend to have gotten wrecked on the jetty rocks. The hull of the ship was washed ashore. No one was aboard. A phenomenal mass of mosquitoes covered the craft. It was days before anyone could investigate what happened. Captain Polk it seems was a pirate in name only, an expatriate not traitor, but not a seeker of the usual bounty. He was investigating folklore that was his life's pursuit.

There is no extended history on him, Only accounts from archivists from that time that followed his life. And those accounts are from tavern wenches and hotel owners that would pretty much spin yarn from here to texas if it would get a few pence out of you. Nothing reliable.

There was some mention, however, about a brief stayover, on Constable Hook, just before he set sail to take on the Key Harbor channel that led to the caverns. He and his small crew stayed at the Olde spye inn, it was mentioned, took up with some whore in conversation by name of Elsie Lodge a common strumpet and con artist. Things got heated over a poor bargaining proposition and the first mate almost had his throat from ear to ear.

He fought off a couple of thugs with his mates and they decided to go back to the ship to avoid any trouble; not looking for any they did not want any it was as simple as that. Captain Horacio Polk and his crew decided to sail off in the middle of the night fearing that they were in danger.

They got as far as the jetty reef when the fog began to cloud over. Trusting only their nautical compass and the tide, they were to just float offshore until the sun came up. Resting, somewhere in between cat naps Polk felt something pulling the boat.

I was pitch black dark, using a few lanterns to light the deck he moved over to the port side of his vessel and threw a slight glow of lantern light over the bow, a halo glow of suppressed moonlight raised its shiny head from behind some black clouds accompanying the scant lantern.

There was a sound of subtle splashing from alongside the boat. It was a flipping sound as though something was swimming parallel broadside. At first, he thought dolphins, but that would have been very unlikely he looked down into the water and spotted something silvery at the port side. As he stared into the water he had the uncanny sensation that something was there. He noticed something silvery again like a pool of tiny shiners feasting on some krill.

Horatio Polk was a seasoned seaman. He was one with the sea. He could sense by the smell coming around that something was not right. Especially the smell he was experiencing; that of a wretched putrid stench of foul decay. He had been at a morgue once to identify a sailor under his command; it was in the new Netherlands, a dirty little city at that time. The sailor was found dead a week after disappearing; what Captain Polk was experiencing was similar to that.

As he looked into the sea, they began to emerge. They were two distinct orbs that were looking at him. They were large and oval as ostrich eggs and did not blink. The pupils were black as the sea nested in a swirling opal mass with a ring of gold glitter encapsulating them. He dared not jump for fear of losing his lantern. He buckled back never taking his eyes off the sea monster staring him down. He reached back for the harpoon gun at the ready to side and gently lifted it from its encasement. With steady aim, he fired point-blank into the head of the creature. The spear went right between the eyes of his target, a direct hit. But nothing happened. The harpoon went right through most likely lodging into the sea bed floor.

The boat held steady as a terrible buzz began to crescendo from the starboard side. He yelled to the first mate but the first mate was drunk. Two other deckhands were wobbling around and one of them made it to his feet, but before Polk could utter a word something grabbed hold of him by his right shoulder digging in with cup-like talons and hoisted him upward, then another flying monstrosity grabbed hold of his leg the same way and in unison, with a jet-like expulsion of strength flew off with the Captain into the darkness.

Within seconds a squad of more creatures came over the ship, taking them away to their cavernous grave. The Tide suddenly erupted, waves of all height breadth and widths began tossing the ship, one deckhand was left he scuttled below throwing any valuables the ship had into a gurney sack, as the ship crashed against the rock he tried in vain to save himself on the rocks. The stones were slippery with moss. A maenad with burning opal eyes sprang from the deep swiping savagely across the sailors' side exposing a kidney to which the creature bit into hungrily, within seconds the man's gizzards were devoured splayed willy-nilly across a flat slab of granite leaving only a wash of blood to intersperse with the strawberry tinted seafoam.

The gurney bag he had flung across his back was severed from his torso and tossed wildly upon the tide.

In the morning as the sun was coming up, reflected light formed a halo around the ships hulk.

There were reports that a tradesmen's ship was wrecked at sea and stranded at the jetty after a freak squall kicked up sometime after midnight. The local sea patrol took a longboat out to examine the wreckage for survivors… but as usual, no one was found, no trace, as though it were a ghost ship.

The reports all coincided that there were tradesmen and crew docked and registered to stay at the Olde spye inn overnight, however, they never made it. After indulging some hard-drinking and uncouth behavior that led to an indecent proposal to the sweet and honorable Elsie Lodge the strangers became drunk and disorderly.

They were escorted back to their ship by some country gentlemen and advised to sleep it off before coming back to the inn.

A leather gurney was washed up on the shore, found by a local passer-by. It was turned over to the patrol and they went through it for identifications. Stuffed in there were journals and maps; diaries of faraway places and Nordic tales of mythology, the paperwork all neatly preserved. Artifacts of that nature; being of no use to alcoholic sea folk, the whole mess was immediately turned over to the local Library where a senior archivist had the good sense to register it with the Library of Congress; and lucky are we for that move on their behalf, The Atlas Yacht club is eternally grateful for that well-intentioned effort.

It seems according to his sketchy notes and some maps that Captain Horatio Polk was following a legend.

It was a legend of the Draugr.

Draugr from what I could find out from my studies combined with what I was able to retrieve from the journals of Polk; gives us a comprehensive understanding of what we are dealing with.

My dear friend. This is going to blow your mind. I only wish we could find Sean Anthony for an Atlas Yacht club meeting… except we need a new clubhouse. And you Charles, are not even allowed to light candles around us anymore.

Well, moving right along.

Read:

Draugr live in their graves, often guarding treasure buried with them in their burial mound. They are animated corpses with a corporeal body, unlike ghosts, with similar physical abilities as in life. Older literature makes clear distinctions between sea-Draugr and land-draugr.

They are embalmed undead corpses of ancient Nords, that was laid to rest a long time ago. Similarly to the undead found in Dummer's tombs on Vvardfel they seem to be guarding the tombs and barrows of ancient Nords across Frozen land.

In the Skaall traditions, some tests send a young Skaal warrior to fight these fierce monsters. By this trial, the young men prove their worthiness and become accomplished members of the Clan.

Draugr possess superhuman strength, can increase their size at will, and carry the unmistakable stench of decay. According to legend, The appearance of a Draugr was that of a dead body: swollen, blackened, and generally hideous to look at. They are undead figures from Norse and Icelandic mythology which appear to retain some semblance of intelligence. They exist to guard their treasure, wreak havoc on living beings, or torment those who wronged them in life. The Draugr's ability to increase its size also increased its weight, and the body of the draugr was described as being extremely versatile. The Myagold of Eybyggia Saga was uncorrupted, and with an ugly look about him… swollen to the size of a large Tuna, and his slippery bulk was so heavy that it could not be raised without levers. They are also noted for the ability to rise from the grave as wisps of smoke and "swim" through solid rock.

In folklore, draugr slay their victims through various methods including crushing them with their enlarged forms, devouring their flesh, devouring them whole in their enlarged forms, indirectly killing them by driving them mad, and by drinking their blood. Animals feeding near the grave of a Draugr might be driven mad by the creature's influence They may also die from being driven mad. myagold, for example, some mutations of these creatures caused birds to drop dead when they flew over his guarded area.

(P.S. I have reason to believe Charles, that these same Myagolds were come to be known later to the Greeks and Romans as Maenads as we have come to know them. Their transformative state may have evolved, in a way the art has evolved and our idea of the human form has evolved over millennia. Margaret might have been thousands of years old when she hooked up; no pun intended with Fitzy, she aged rapidly from being out of the water to care for Aggie.)

Read on:
The Draugr victims were not limited to trespassers in its home; the roaming undead devastated livestock, by running the animals to

death, either by riding them or pursuing them in some hideous, half-flayed form. A gatekeepers duties kept them outdoors at night, and they were particular targets for the hunger and hatred of the undead:

The slaves which had been used to haul Myagold bodies were ridden to death by demons, and every single beast that came near his grave went raving mad and howled itself to death. The gatekeeper onshore often came racing back to port with Myagold after him. One day that Fall neither ship nor sailor came back to the sea.

Draugr is noted for having numerous magical abilities (referred to as [trollskap] they are said to resemble those of living witches and wizards, some magic they employ are in the forms of shape-shifting, controlling the weather, and seeing into the future. A draugr can change into a mermaid, a raven, a grey wolf with a broken back but no ears or tail, and a cat that would sit upon a sleeper's chest and grow steadily heavier until the victim suffocated. The draugr shape-shifted and could change into wolf-like creatures.

The males could become insects or other flying creatures, such as Mosquitoes or large bats. At times disguised beings resembling impish men or troll-like animations, They brought with them a horrible stench; a corrosive odor that could throw their victims into a convulsive state of nausea, thus distracting, enabling the predator to make its strike. The male would stick his claw-like fingers into the neck, tearing the flesh and sinew from his bones with deadly accuracy.

Draugr can enter into the dreams of the living and they will frequently leave a gift behind so that "the living person may be assured of the tangible nature of the visit sometimes trinkets or glass stones. Draugr also can curse a victim, as shown in the Ghita saga, where Ghita is cursed to be unable to become any stronger.

Draugr also brought disease to a village and could create temporary darkness in daylight hours. They preferred to be active during the night, although it did not appear to be vulnerable to sunlight like some other revenants. Draugr can also kill people with bad luck.

A Draugr presence might be shown by a great light that glowed from the mound like volcano fire. This fire would form a barrier between the land of the living and the land of the dead. The draugr could also move magically through the earth, swimming through solid stone.

Some draugr are immune to weapons, and only a hero has the strength and courage needed to stand up to so formidable an opponent. In legends, the hero would often have to wrestle the draugr back to his grave, thereby defeating him, since weapons would do no good. (P.S. *A good example of this Charles is when you told the story of how Aggie shot a Maenad with the harpoon at your first encounter... It had no physical effect. The effect was purely psychological; Yet the maenad knew it was being shot at by Aggie, a worthy opponent (hero)- and backed off.)*

Read on my brother:

Iron could injure a draugr, as is the case with many supernatural creatures, although it would not be sufficient to stop it. Sometimes the hero is required to dispose of the body in unconventional ways. The preferred method is to cut off the draugr head, burn the body, and dump the ashes in the sea—the emphasis being on making sure that the draugr was dead and gone.

The draugr were said to be either ("death-blue") or ("corpse-pale"). The death-blue color was not grey but was a dark blue or maroon hue which covered the entire body Olde Fitzy, the blown-out old salt that he was, was an unusually dark blue, I half-seen corpses in some biology classes I had on forensics during my studies at peck Mont and I can tell you he was not typical.

Some legends describe how bones were dug up belonging to dead sorceresses who had appeared in dreams, and they were - "blue and evil-looking."

The resting place of the draugr was a tomb in which they were able to leave during the night to visit the living. Such visits are supposed to be horrible events that often end in death for one or more of the living, which would then warrant the exhumation of the draugr by a hero.

The draugr motivation was primarily jealousy and greed. Greed causes it to viciously attack any would-be grave robbers, but the draugr also expresses innate jealousy of the living stemming from a longing for the things of life which it once had.

The main indication that a deceased person will become a draugr is that the corpse is not in a horizontal position but is found in an upright or sitting position, indicating that the dead might return. Any mean, nasty, or greedy person can become a draugr; as you must have noticed in my notes, Charles. Most archaic myths and monsters were evil or unhappy mortals at one time or another. If not dissatisfied or evil, they were most likely not the ones to be voted most popular by the Roman bath committee or other such popular franchises.

The funeral rite is interpreted as having a "grave binding inscription" used to keep the deceased in its grave.

Traditionally, a pair of open iron scissors was placed on the chest of the recently deceased, along with straws or twigs that might be hidden among their clothes. The big toes were tied together or needles were driven through the soles of the feet to keep the dead from being able to walk. Tradition also held that the coffin should be lifted and lowered in three different directions as it was carried from the house to confuse a possible draugr sense of direction.

The most effective means of preventing the return of the dead was believed to be a corpse door, a special door through which the corpse was carried feet-first with people surrounding it so that the corpse couldn't see where it was going. The door was then bricked up to prevent a return. It is speculated that this belief began in Denmark and spread throughout the Norse culture, founded on the idea that the dead could only leave through the way they entered.

(P.S. I can't help thinking Charlie of the wunder Krammer on the moon cursor and how I was so enthralled that night. Do you think it was a trick to captivate me? I mean you saw it too didn't you. And what about Aggies Library in the Belltower? Were you able to look over the books and journals; perhaps purloin a slim volume of poetry that you are not telling us about? Anything that might add another piece to this puzzle would be helpful. How about Aggie's letters, surely she must have written you love letters of some kind, Was there anything like a romantic love between you two, or was it just Dark arcadia, and gothic doom and gloom?

C'mon Charlie, now is the time to fess up, you spent a lot of time in that bell tower, we are grown men Charles, The hour for gentlemanly decorum has passed, this is history now, what is a maenad like under the sheets? Did you smack the monkey or not? A true confession on our behalf, Sean Anthony told me that on one occasion during a meeting, he saw her nipple due to a clothing malfunction. He said it looked normal. Did she ever try to bite you?

As always,

Your Magister Ludi. John Morris

I have to admit I did not like his particular line of questioning. I have always respected Aggie and because of the dark hard secrets in her life, I have always tried to protect her from uncomforted embarrassment. I particularly never liked the way John was always trying to find out more about Aggie in a romantic way. He had a crush on her that was obvious even Aggie was aware of it, but no one ever made an issue of it. Just sometimes the prickly thorns of envy became evident, as with these slippery little innuendoes disguised as club business.

I let it go then and I will continue to let it go.

I had never done well in college dating. I thought that what Aggie and I had those few summers was a dark study in a romance that even for an impressionable kid was a little strange. Like everything else about that place, it was a cyclical, emotional tide that rushed in and rushed out. Never enough time to make roots. Like a Viking or a modern Odysseus accept with Aggie it was in reverse. She was the bell tower, tide and circumstance oscillated around her. Our attempts at lovemaking like most nerdy teenagers were bumbling and stupid, nothing was ever consummated on those breezy afternoons in the bell tower, nothing I would have to worry about if Fitzy walked wanting to behead me. Besides, there were the jealous maenads to think about. That female one that was not so fond of me; of all things to contend with, a flesh-eating, lesbian mermaid has a crush on my girlfriend and the Magister Ludi wants to know about my love life. There were a few occasions when I would visit Key Harbor during winter-breaks and bring Aggie to my parent's summer home, We had complete privacy, and we were much older.

I had been taking some biology classes that year, and some elementary questions about female composition were introduced to me neatly in clear concise textbook jargon, in graphic detail even our Magister Ludi John Morris would be comfortable with.

All kidding aside, Aggie was astonishing that year. She had developed into an incredible woman. She came to the cottage. I was arranging some things to make the place less stuffy. She rode her bike up the macadam driveway lying it still against the house. For once I was observing her from my domain. She was dressed in the most flowing lace skirt with denim draped around, she was up casually held loosely with a pin. No makeup but Aggie never needed any. A natural beauty; Celtic, Dane, and Dutch framed her bone structure but her eyes were Maenad. The eyes were wide and elliptical enchanting to look into, even from a distance I see clear like glass and green not wild and forbidding as I remembered them at the bell tower. As she got close, a scent of lavender and sage permeated from her a natural exuberance from someone happy to see me. No. Nothing from scratched out journal pages was going to defeat this day, it was ours.

I opened the door and she stepped inside and we hugged. My head a rushing whirl in deep confusion. "Welcome". I said. She curtseyed.

Most of the idle chit chat that took up the minutes and hours of that day went unnoted, I won't bore you with details, only that at some point she was standing still in front of me lost in thought statuesque, like art forcing me to look closer and I went to her. We kissed, and we kissed again longer this time, we fell onto the couch and I half opened my eyes to catch her looking into me. If I could recall the painting, I cannot, only that it was an English painter I believe, that added a high-light so delicate on to a woman's eye on this one fine portrait I recall; in that single stroke there was no mistaking it to be a tear of happiness and surrender.

Her flesh was pliable and emollient cool to the touch, satisfying and soothing. I was afraid to disturb it with clumsy touching and moving. I kissed gently across her face, slowly along her arms as not to disturb one goosebump until My butterfly kisses came to rest on breasts.

Our hunger knew no boundaries, we swelled and heaved, undulating with each living pulse. New blood rushed to my temples as I looked into her eyes one more. This, however, still yet a new sensation. Those orbs of green-blue a shade that would bring envy to the sea were now swirling, the same whirlpool of opal flame I remember seeing briefly on my first meeting with Aggie that day on the beach. So instantaneous was it, I had thought I imagined it. She was as excited then as she is now… she had always desired me; and me, her.

After we made love there was no room emotionally for words. We held hands and rested I believe she had known better than I that she had given me a gift I could never keep; Herself. But what was I to do with it? Suddenly a frost of chilling deja vu came over me..not a recalled memory exactly, more like a telepathic memory.

It was that maenad, the first time I was at the bell tower, how it whispered to me; the smell, the sweat, and pine needles…it groused, with that cracking voice "And what was it worth to worry and where did it go"

It mocked me. That lesbian maenad sent a subliminal precursory note to my destiny… knowing I had no future with Aggie it mocks me, what evil creatures these are. I looked over to her in panic, afraid that everything we just found would disappear; she was napping angelic like a child. Looking at her I could only feel love the one antidote that levies these toxic creatures. I rested my head in her embrace and drifted off with the smell of lavender sage and wildflowers comforting me.

A reading from John; Our brother in arms the Magister Ludi from the Atlas yacht club and rude individual.

Spank the monkey indeed.

In *Eyrbyggja saga*, Draugar are driven off by holding a "door-doom". One by one, they are summoned to the door-doom and given judgment and forced out of the home by this legal method. The home was then purified with holy water to ensure that they never came back.

A variation of the draugr is the Myagold hagaurus (from Old Norse *hagr'* (hag) which was a mound-dweller, the dead body living on within its tomb. The notable difference between the two was that the hagaurus is unable to leave its gravesite and only attacks those who trespass upon their territory.

(This is it Charlie… the caverns. Some of those creatures never left the caverns. They were dead bodies living on in those underground catacombs. The mystery of the moon cursor was that it was a body trafficking ghost machine. The Good princess supplied bounty to the undead existing in the caverns. They feasted on the blood of the juicy mosquitoes. And probably; cats, dogs, and missing persons. The mosquitoes bred mosquitos. They were keeping those bloodthirsty vampires out of the limelight by feeding them those huge mosquitos. This tradition was being carried out for millennia on end.

Aggie was a freak to them, as well as a freak to us. She did not fit in anywhere. They were grooming her to be the custodian over the caverns. The Sea Hag was her destiny. This might explain why Margaret married Fitzy. She needed a child. It was Margaret all along, I believe that possessed the Moon cursor she was controlling Fitzy therein. Fitzy might be alive in that cavern somewhere, an undead. (Who knows what his role in all of this was.)

Read on… sorry about that statement concerning Aggie, I know you guys were close. You know I am not good with social graces.

Closing statement;

The Myagold was rarely found far from its burial place and is a type of undead commonly found in Norse sagas. The creature is said to either swim alongside boats or sail around them in a partially submerged vessel, always on their own. In some accounts, witnesses portray them as shapeshifters who take on the appearance of seaweed or moss-covered stones on the shoreline.

Bingo.

I paced around my room after reading this letter. It was the last I received from John Morris. I am not sure if the administration here started screening my mail or he just stopped writing. I hope he never went back to Constable Hook. He would be insane to even think of doing so. But his curiosity got us to figure out a little of what has happened to us and why.

Sean Anthony.

It was a bell, a bell big and rings on. Sean Anthony turned off the corner of a four-post bed gently pulling back a lacey curtain. A view, from the window, painted a picture of pedestrian frailty huddled against the cold and damp; racing through and around Thin puddles forming under and in between cobblestone embankments. The rain has subsided, umbrellas are closing and the cafes are filling up with undernourished souls making do with their morning coffee.

Thin whiff of smoke rolls over his shoulder like a snake to curl under his nose like a warm friend. From the corner of his eye, he addresses the shadow of a woman." Did you sleep well? He asked. "Wonderfully well" she exudes.

The shadow still in his peripheral sight crooks an arm to almost a salute position, he could tell she is applying her eyelashes that are quite lengthy.

"What are your plans today sailor boy?" Her English is quite good, with an accent of heavy Dutch.

"I will be setting up shop here for a while, I need to find a place, maybe in the lower quarter. I will be doing artwork, so it does not have to be anything fancy. The more inconspicuous the better."

"I have some friends that work in inexpensive neighborhoods. I could bring you around if you don't mind the area code; As Americans say."

"I don't mind the area code."

The shadow moved, now her back was arched her head pushed forward into the mirror. the elbow tucked in and steady. She was putting on her lipstick.

After a few puckers and pops, she was ready to converse again.

"At three o'clock, meet me at the coffee shop on Erlanger. There is only one, you should have no trouble finding it."

"Alright".

The shadow now elongated into a full standing figure. Sean Anthony rose from the bed and walked over to her addressing her in the full morning light.

"Have a good day Sasha, don't work too hard."

"See you at three Sean, don't forget."

"I will be there, My treat,"

"Of course."

He held her neck and kissed her gently on the forehead.

"OHHH", she purred, with wanting eyes.

"Your lipstick"… he said.

With her hand on her hip, she shifted her weight to the left leg.

"You are too kind"

He playfully tapped her bum as she exited.

Sean Anthony walked back toward the window pulled back the lace curtain one more time. The sun was now coming out and the rain had cleared up completely. Sasha had left the building and was crossing the street. She went to the corner of Vanpool and made a right disappearing into the mix.

Sean Anthony thought to himself, this is the last fine hotel I will be staying at for a while.

It wore on him very heavily not to have killed Sasha last night. He could feel her blood rushing to the surface, as they made love. He could hear her heart pumping like that Big brass church bell. With every thrust, his temples crashed with blood lust. He went over to the mirror and looked into it deeply, His eyes were a deep mud color of complex sepia and greens, The beginning swirls of excitement began to activate in his iris anticipating a celebratory blood feast. But, "I must wait… there is work to be done. Protocol as American maenads says.

I could take my leave in Amsterdam without any problems from the merchant maritime commission. When I wish to leave I can report to the maritime union office and apply for the next freight out. This luncheon at three o'clock will determine my next three months.

The clock on the wall, read at three o'clock. Sasha came into the café with a gaunt man who looked around sixty or so, he was most likely younger, people rarely make it to sixty around here, the decadence is intense.

"Sean I am glad to see you, Happy you made it." Sasha flashed a big smile of pearly whites, with her arm gently around the man; she introduced.

"Sean this is Pieter, Pieter Sean."

I nudged slightly in my seat adjusting my posture more than anything. I didn't particularly care for formalities and this man was a bit unsavory for such a nice day.

The man was somewhat abrupt cutting to the quick without any red tape.

Sash tells me you are looking for a room with no-frills, fairly large is that correct Mr. I apologize I don't believe I got your last name. "Anthony"

"yes she told me you are an artist is that correct?

"Yes."

"You are American?"

"Yes sir"

"Let me come right to the point Mr. Anthony. We are speaking because Sasha recommended you. I have to be assured that no nefarious business will take place in the form of manufacturing or distributing any kind of narcotic. Americans and other expatriates come to this section of Amsterdam for many reasons. If I seem a bit brass, it is because I cannot have any problems with the police. So allow me to cut to the quick. If there is anything that might bring a problem of the sort I just mentioned, it would be wise for you to tell me now or things could get uncomfortable. So, with that being said, do you have any problems with narcotics Mr. Anthony?"

"No, sir I do not."

"Good."

"Are you hiding from the police; American or otherwise?"

"No Sir."

"One more thing. Mr. Anthony, The girls that you see in the building work for me. Please keep that in mind. You may see or hear things that could disturb you. I hope that you act accordingly. You must be discreet with some of their clients you might recognize; Am I clear on that?"

Yes sir, I understand.

"Alright then, I know you work for the maritime and have an income What you do with your art is your own business. I assure you you will find an ample amount of models if you need them, as long as they are paid."

A sinister smile crawled across his face as he stood up just as abruptly as he spoke. He continued.

"I have given the key and instructions to Sasha, she will close this out, you can communicate with me through her, or contact my direct, she has all the information. If there is anything I can assist you with, within your endeavors, do contact me, I have many connections in Amsterdam, some of which are in the art world. Let me know if I can be of any service.

With that, he dropped a key into Sasha's hand and whispered something into her ear. Then turned and hailed a taxi.

Sasha and I remained seated as a waiter came to the table. I ordered a croissant and coffee Sasha ordered the same.

I watched Pieter walk toward the cab, his open cashmere coat buckling against the breeze; a lock of salt and pepper gray hair lifting from his brow. He wore linen trousers… compelled I was, to refer to a man's pants as trousers but that's how elegant they were. Everything about him flowed in a kind European poetry.

Sasha looked at me grabbing both my hand from across the table.

"You got it"! She said. "I am so happy. You know it could have gone either way Pieter, is a difficult person to win over."

"Is that right?"? I answered. "Why so?"

"Pieter is an independent businessman. He can be ruthless. On your own, you would have never gotten that room. Or even ever heard of him for that matter. He is what you might say in America; an underground character."

You don't say, I take it you two are close, more than just business associates. Would he have a problem if he knew, we were fucking: and not just in the mutual courtesan John relationship.

"I don't know what you mean?"

"I am entertaining the thought we have a different sort of relationship. You have been staying over, not charging me. I make you breakfast, we share soul secrets, I don't do that with everyone. Your intimacies make me feel special. If I am mistaken, please correct me now before I commit to something irrational."

-"Like falling in love?"

"I would like to think love is more than just sticking it in and Cumming. Sean answered.

"You mean, like falling in Love?" Sasha repeated.

I suppose. How do you feel about that?"

"I am already there."

"That being said, how would Pieter feel about this; is what I am getting at," Sean asked again.

Sasha was cool and collected. She knew that this was a problem looming behind the curtain.

Sasha looked up from her coffee for the first time; she continued stirring the spoon gently tapping the sides of the cup.

"He is testing me, this little episode of him handing me the key and giving me complete access to you…it's a dare don't you see?"

"He knows about us?"

"He suspects. Do not most men have antennae that go up when a potential threat walks into the room? I know women do." For instance, I can sense that you are looking at that young girl's ass behind me as she fumbles to drape her coat around her chair. Even though you are wearing those dark glasses that conceal your eyes. I just know. Am I wrong?"

"I notice her," Sean said.

Sasha leaned back and smiled like the Cheshire cat.

"Should a woman, take a chance on a romance as serious as this, with a man that is so easily distracted?"

"You are avoiding the question about Pieter; I don't want anything to happen to you."

"Pieter is a big boy, I am expendable," Sasha said leaning back into her chair.

It was his move. He dared not remove his sunglasses. His irises were swirling with violent opal fire rage. He could feel it. He wanted to taste her. The intensity for her blood was becoming more than the desire to ravish her body of all its sensual pleasures. This is what he was afraid of; this is what he did not want to happen.

He thought it was going to be quick. A meeting with a hooker; in a strange country, a seedy part of town; two strangers. He could take her to his hotel, suck her blood, destroy her leave her empty, and abscond. But something happened, a cognitive dissonance disrupted the game plan. He could not kill her. He would at some point have to make her like him if this was ever going to happen. He could not go back. It was almost a month now into their relationship. And every day the feeling got more intense.

To make matters worse Sean Anthony was changing also, physically but mostly psychologically. He was not the same as he was back at home. All innocence was leaving him. A yearning to return to the sea was festering in him. This maenad disease was changing him. What he had detested, what he found gross in them was becoming attractive. How frail and lovely Sasha was. This very human trait was so sweet to him. He indeed needed to taste her.

They went back to the hotel and clawed each other like tigers. The stronger his desire to bite and suck at her became, the more brutally and passionately Sean penetrated; when the ritual was over. They lay temporarily purged of their lust. Sasha observed Sean watching through the mirror as she brushed her hair; the distance between them was not so great in that small room. She thought him an unusual creature, magnificent in some way…so much so she must have imagined his eyes had a golden speck infused in them, like the eye of a wild animal. The mirror was old and the reflective qualities were not so good…but still those eyes with hues of soft browns and painterly greens seemed to be moving. Sasha thought Sean's eyes were hazel in direct sunlight. But the iris's seemed to be changing tint at points in time, like that of the sea when tides change under influence of the rising and setting sun.

After dressing Sean came up behind her, nestling his face in her hair. She still could not get a clear look at those eyes; Sasha pulled the keys from her purse and dangled them in front of the mirror hoping he would lookup.

Well, let's go visit your new studio room. She said, dangling the keys, hoping to catch a full frontal gaze at his face.

Sean looked up and his eyes were, brown. Just large cow-like big brown eyes like the day they first met on that avenue almost a month ago, how things have changed. She must have imagined it she thought, just nerves playing tricks. They left the room and giggled down the hallway like two excited children.

We taxied to the other end of town to a much more seedy section. The main streets and thoroughfares were well lighted and brash like any other commercial avenue however, once off the beaten path things got off the mainstream fast.

Sasha knew her way around. We leaped over puddles and went around overturned trash cans. Some women dressed in strange combinations of trendy fashion waved us on. There were all types of people. We came to the building and stopped. The sign on the door read Oost Fierserstaat. There were people outside looking at us. They seemed to know Sasha but she did not acknowledge them. As we made our way to the back of the building it was clear people got out of the way for Sasha. She had clout here. No doubt due to her affiliation with Pieter. When we came to the end of a long hallway Sasha opened a large wooden door. It unfolded into the room I had rented.

It was much more spacious than I had expected.

"Wow, this is cool," he said.

Sasha remained silent.

The room was an abandoned cafeteria. Plenty of space to paint and what's more so lots of storage I could easily live in it, I could get a makeshift bed, and there appeared to be an industrial kitchen space, bathroom, and running water. The window was a high skylight window that stretched across the ceiling. Some chains hung from a pulley with a brass handle, to open and close. In New York, this would be a fortune.

"Tomorrow we must go shopping. "he told Sasha, "I will need some supplies, I believe there is an art supply store over on Utrecht."

"But tonight we will celebrate, what was that place we passed on the way up here, with the stained glass windows and big doors?"

"It is called the pyre; it is a kind of night club, is that where you want to go, Sean?"

"Of course, I am not so old that I cannot enjoy a strange brew..."

Sasha laughed, knowing that the age difference between them would have to be addressed at some point in the relationship. However, after seeing Pieter, Sean was convinced that older men were of no consequence to Sasha. Sean had a New York cool that held up. Sasha was somewhere in her mid-twenties. Her lifestyle made her look somewhat older, however, She was ridiculously too young for Pieter who thought of himself as the quintessential ladies man with his silver hair and Prada suit. Sean Anthony not that much older pushing forty.

With that, they scuttled over to the PYRE.

As they approached the PYRE a strange feeling of Déjà vu came over Sean Anthony. The crest motif that was reoccurring on the inlaid stained glass was disturbing. They were mermaids poised and shrunken of a different kind. They looked very similar to maenads. They were typical mermaids as one would expect to see except that the heads were that of a medusa with snakes and serpents; the teeth were fang-like and ominous.

The crowd outside was young; leather and Celt plaid wrapped around the waist seemed to be popular for both men and women.

The boots reminded him of the Magister Ludi. How he wished John Morris could see this place. This would be the kind of place they could talk about The horror, An Atlas Yacht club away from home…

The frail young women were telling stories in dark tattoos and painful-looking piercings. Sudden arousal began to stir like the smell of blood. This was new, new sensations were manifesting more frequently lately. In a brief panic, he searched for Sasha, she was at the entrance gate making an arrangement to get in.

The man at the door stopped the line of customers waiting to get in and kissed Sasha on both cheeks, Sasha called over to Sean Anthony absorbed in the stained glass.

"Sean. C'mon,"

Sasha had an influence. No doubt about it. it also was becoming more clear, that at some point, Pieter was going to be a force to be reckoned with.

No one relinquishes this much power to someone and then lets them just walk away with any new kid in town. Sasha is not telling the whole story. There is a danger here.

They went inside and got a table for two, a brass rail stretched across a parallel wall. Some sconces hung overhead.

"We will sit here. A good vantage point, you could see who is going and coming." -Said Sasha.

The floor was slightly elevated along the perimeters of the room. We had to climb three steps or so. In front of us, a long wooden table extended through the middle of the room it was littered with glass bottles and debris. At the end of it was a huge fireplace. Indeed a pyre looking fire pit. It was blazing.

Sitting along both sides left and right of the slab were the patrons mostly male. They adorned Jackets of leather stressed across broad backs. Some skinny burn-outs slumped over their ale in a half stupor. A few had cargo pants with chains dangling from their belt loops.

They looked estranged and menacing like Hell's Angles but there were no colors on their backs or no sign of motor-cycles, Sasha informed that these were your local brand of Gothic knights; disenfranchised Voodoo children who roam the countryside drunk and disorderly; a youthful fraternity of brotherhood whom I Sean Anthony had always wished I were a part of.

I Sean Anthony have never been part of a softball team, have joined a league of any sort. Studying art was lonely and to be frank about it, artists rarely hang out with other artists… They wind up hating each other.

The girls were scattered about to each their own playing up to their own Goth fantasy. The caked-on war paint of gray rouge contrasted against the pale white skin of the Dutch fall season.

Snaking eyes from slits of Nefertiti mascara nictitate, adding to the scene making it dreamlike and fantastic. Sean Anthony and Sasha held hands in the dark. The club lighting neutralized his eyes temporarily so he could speak freely looking into sash's warm orb discernments without fear of her noticing his blood lust zoom warming up.

They spoke of Sean's plans and some of their dreams. Sasha had never been so excited. She sensed a change something that could change her life, perhaps get her out of this New Amsterdam ghetto.

There was no romance here for her. She was what Pieter kept her as a dumb whore.

Their relationship was unholy from the start. Sash's father who was killed was a made man, with an underground mob in Amsterdam that Pieter was a part and parcel. It was never clear what happened. Her father worked with Pieter running some questionable operations. Pieter was a low man on the totem pole. Some plans went wrong Pieter sold out and Sasha's father was killed in a mysterious car accident. Pieter was promoted to a higher position in the organization and has been rising ever since. He is now very powerful and has Sasha doing his bidding for him.

Sasha was sixteen when she was adopted by Pieter kept her as his courtesan, kind of a trophy. And an example to those under him, proving this kind of ruthlessness is what you can expect if you betray him. Sasha never dreamed of getting away. She was sure she was to die at an early age like her father, probably on the anniversary of his death, Pieter might kill her to complete his vendetta, which was coming soon; another peccadillo of his ruthlessness. Either way, Sasha was prepared to die.

Sasha knows she is being set up and that Sean is being duped. She will tell him. She is going to Tell Sean Anthony, everything, and hope he can think of a way to get them both out of the country.

She knows there is one way to get away from him, away from it all, Pieter van Groit must die.

The chemistry and physical make-up of the Atlas yacht club boys at the time of their banning together could not have been more different, and yet they were similar in simple passions that bonded them in their unique pursuits. They were not unlike a rock –band guided by a primitive instinct to stay dedicated to a holy barbaric cause; invisible and unexplainable yet coalesced by a love of semiotic images and ancient adages that assuaged the chaotic hemorrhages of awkward youth; meaning they could star out in their way without having to waver in favor of conformity. They could form an identity and carry a" mojo" inside themselves, a talisman by which each one could draw a line in the sand asserting to the philistines at the gate… "This line you do not cross."

The medium for this manifesto was Literature. What john Morris brought to the table was dark of course, And I must confess I loved his stories the best on those Misty harbor nights. The light from the bell tower accenting the moon cursor as it bobbed and rocked against the pilings; caustic ochre lights illuminating from Captain Fitzy's cabin, where he lay awake under house arrest by the moon cursor.

And each of us; I, The Magister Ludi and Sean Anthony huddled around novena candles that we stole from home; permanently borrowed from our mothers who always kept a box somewhere in the house in case of an electrical outage.

It wasn't until Aggie unleashed the horror on us that we understood this gruesome place. And what it had in store for us.

What we were like in those days was not without its flavor and charm.

The Magister Ludi; John Morris for example,(and there could be no better example), was in character something of a pagan. A spectator from the outside world might denote him as an eccentric. I know now that he was and is a maniac; not in the sense that he would hurt anyone he would not, he was most benevolent actually, He would just exhibit symptoms of wild behavior. I know now that his teenage years were pent up with anxiety and boredom, which was probably one reason his parents brought him to Key Harbor every summer, to get him acclimated to social adjustment. Water seeks its level, He found the Atlas Yacht club.

John Morris, or "Magister Ludi", has formulated his fantasy so well that the persona of "odd, mystic wizard" has remained with him still into his middle age and then some. Over the decades you might say he has morphed into a grungy steampunk hipster sort of character intensely intellectual; a gray bat, that hangs around the halls of dark academia with quill pen and skull of memento mori. He remains To this day a stoic of classical antiquity. Forever, with a notebook in his hand jotting quotes from Lord Byron and James Russel Lowell.

Not ever to be mistaken as handsome, the Ludi had a look of what one might define as archetypal in a gothic way; the russet ringlet hair and a square face, broad at the shoulders and somewhat barreled about the chest and mid-section like a monk. The first image conjured up by anyone at a university would be saintly or philosophical; brandishing long coats and leather satchels. His musical taste spanned from, Tchaikovsky (mostly, The USSR Ministry of culture chamber choir) variety to incomprehensible grunge and heavy metal. He was quite strong despite his gnome appearance when we threw Fitzy onto the caverns that night, he handled the dead weight mostly himself, I must confess, Sean Anthony and I were of little help.

Sean Anthony was a whimsical poet with a paintbrush. He was thin and Lanky as a teenager, with the faraway look of an artist of some type. He weaved nicely into everyone's fantasies and brought a certain careless elegance into the Olde spye inn. All of our furniture and almost all of the wall décor was provided by Sean Anthony. He was a notorious dumpster diver with an eye for great stuff. He found plaster busts of Elvis along with all kinds of boardwalk fanfare that tourists would trash over the years. We had crazy drapes from summer homes and coffee pots, cots with makeshift mattresses and cups goblets, books, and of course porn magazines. Sean Anthony was not a nerd like we were. He was more streetwise and entertaining. We all came from the suburbs or soft cities, his folks brought him in from exotic places like Chicago, the Bronx, and New Orleans. His dad Came from Jersey City, New Jersey, and had a high-level gig in sales that took them all over the place. But they always vacationed back at Key harbor, partly because his folks liked it there I guess and because Sean Anthony liked the Atlas Yacht club meetings, bitching them to go back.

He never said much at the meetings, he just kind of cracked jokes and told stories at the yacht club most of which were more like the lives of artists. Sometimes he would spring an obscure poet on us and that was fun. With that being said, what he lacked in intellectual contribution. he more than made up for bringing porn magazines.

So what can I get you from the bar? Sean Anthony asked

"They make a drink here called the gliding Griffin, I will have one of those," Sasha said.

Sean Anthony could not focus on drinks; his head was turned by the scent of a waif-like nymph that was standing over the table talking to a hard-rocking nihilist. He handed her something that was rolled up like a cigarette and she pecked his cheek and turned back to her friends.

Sean Anthony went to the bar to order. He placed his order for a beer and a gliding Griffin. He watched the bartender pour what seemed to be an equal amount of Irish mist whiskey and amaretto then top it with a soda. They applied something that made it smoke but was too distracted to see what it was. He was watching the punk girls getting goofy with her friends. The smell of blood was different as it crossed the room. Almost like designer cologne in a room full of cheap powder water brands.

He brought the drinks back to the table and things got normal again. Sasha told him she was going to leave she had to get back for reasons she did not disclose.

"Sean, here you have your keys, I am going back to my place, I will drop in tomorrow morning and we can go shopping for your supplies. I will see you then."

She kissed him and left, he walked out with her and stayed until she hailed a taxi, something was brewing Sean stayed for a little while longer at the Pyre. The girl he was watching had left. He watched her part from some friends and head through a park along the old canal. Sean followed. The girl checked her watch and sat on a bench. She was waiting for someone. Sean began quaking and shivering he felt his face it was numb something was changing. He went into a dry sweat.

The girl took the cigarette that she got from the kid at the bar and placed it between her lips and lit it. She took a long drag, there was silence by the canal except for a form breathing down on her from behind. In a second her neck was snapped. The last thing she recalled while still warm before death came to call was damp lips sucking at her throat.

It did not take long. In a few seconds, Sean ripped through her scantily clad body quite easily. He gobbled hungrily; trotting off in the form of a diseased vagrant. Disappearing in the park then trotted back to the Oost fierstaat.

Once back in the room he fell on the floor and slept almost unconscious until Sasha came knocking the next day.

The frantic knocking woke him up.

He had an unpleasant sleep like one would experience under chemical-induced anesthesia such as ether, inducing hallucinogenic dreams in florescent chemical colors. He dreamt he was a sleeping giant like that in Gulliver's travels tied by cords on a wooden slab much like the table at Pyre. The background was completely black. Only his animated self-lit up, like a cartoon and a small dwarf-like creature wearing a multicolored cone hat. The little man was carrying a large mallet shaped hammer and walked along his stomach; the elf-like creature stopped at his chest looking down on him sleeping. With that the little man clutched the hammer with both hands and struck Sean Anthony's forehead three times, releasing a firework display of florescent orange, hot pinks, and cobalt blues…the knocking in his head awoke him, it took a few seconds to realize someone was pounding at the door.

Familiarizing himself with the conscious world, he took a moment.

The pounding door frightened him he thought he might have been followed from last night's kill, A panic ran through him. The voice on the other end low and desperate.

"Sean it's me open…"

He opened the door to greet Sasha, who was a beaten mess.

"Sasha, My God, slowly, what happened? Who did this to you?"

Sean, it is Pieter, He has us set up, My time is up with him, I was meant to be killed, but I escaped, He has some terrible things planned, he is a sadistic maniac. That is what this place is all about, he means to torture and kills us here. It is something that goes way back Ido not have time to explain, you must go hurry, I am dying, I think. His thugs worked me over pretty good. Go he will be here very soon, if not now, I am going to die, I am bleeding from everywhere.

Her soft warm blood was sweet. He ran his fingers through her bloody hair and kissed sweet blood off her face.

The thumping sound in the hall was getting loud. They were here; Showtime!

Sean Anthony was satiated from last night's kill. But the sweetness of Sasha's blood invigorated him enough to explore his newfound talent the will to change form. Sean began to figure out that when you become excited you can do things more quickly. You learn as you go along, sort of like sex. The lust comes over you, you become lost in the process, and as a result you kind of figure your body out.

Note to self. 0x/ 0x / wedn.

For no apparent reason, a story The Magister Ludi told us once at an Atlas Yacht club meeting about a kid he knew in school, that had an orgasm climbing a rope in gym class I don't know that just popped into my head just before I am about to massacre some evil people.

I wonder how long I am going to live. If my infection of this maenad thing leads me to crave water might have to go into the sea or age quickly, or I might be a land type. This maenad thing is a whole new learning game. For example, Sas…! To be continued.

The excitement and panic were driving him. He felt the heaves of dry sweat rising from his gut. His mind was clearer than it was last night; killing that steampunk chick. His first real kill: His body strong from nourishment, a tremble came over him as the steps got close. He took Sasha who was still pumping blood and rested her against the wall; she grew weaker every second. The lifeblood was spilling out of her and puddling onto the floor. He kissed her one last time as a human, and then turning toward the door he unlocked it and undid the chain latch. So they can enter, untethered.

Pieter Van Griot and two thugs stood outside the door. Pieter turned the knob slowly pushing it open ever so slowly. Knowing Sasha had tipped off Sean, Sean most likely exited by the window and was on his way back to the mariner's marine office ready to go out on the next Job; all part of the plan. The three goons stood in the room facing Sasha who was near death, and struggling for breath. Pieter walked to an open window where a breeze was blowing a tattered curtain. He looked outside onto the fire escape, there was nothing?

I had told you my dear that your friend would leave you. You see, to him, you are his whore, to me you are my wife. To see you laying there bleeding you remind me so much of your father. He betrayed me also. And now my vendetta is fulfilled. From the skylight above shadows splaying across the room. A Raven, A monstrous Raven was perched on the edge of the skylight frame. In a moment it swooped down landing both claws into the eyes of Pieter blinding him instantly; ricocheting it flew headlong into Pieter's thug jamming his eye and socket with a tremendous beak. The last thug head for the door as he reached to unlock it his wrist was pecked opening up a vein spurting blood like a fountain. He pulled a blade from his jacket with his other hand and waved it wildly in the air unable to strike his relentless attacker. He was pecked about the head and neck until he succumbed to the pommeling jabs. Pieter lay huddled in the corner holding his hands over empty sockets crying, but to no avail; tears were not to be formed from destroyed eyeballs and tear ducts. The raven then circled him and pushed the mighty beak into the soft side of Pieter's temple crushing it once and for all.

The bird hovered over to where Sasha lay and perched by her side. In a few minutes, it transformed back to Sean Anthony. Sasha was almost dead, there was no time to negotiate or explain his case. He took her gently into his hands and bit into her. The slow pulsing lifeblood is mostly diffused unto the floor. She winced, when she comes around to awakening state, Sean Anthony must get her to the river where she can be baptized, which means water from the sea must enter her lungs as if drowning causing her to die twice so she can become a maenad as Aggie was.

Sean could never become like her again, the only way to save her was to make her like him. (She will have to hunt blood now as I do.) We must live in secret. Will we love as we did? I don't know... I do know she loved me out of emotion and I was lusting her blood, how will that play out? I don't know. Surly love will not be an issue we will not want each other. We will crave strangers. A different type of jealousy and sense of possession might ensue. We are starting new. She will have a new life. One underpinning of uncertainty hangs over our heads; If she craves the sea, she might have to go to the ocean like a true maenad… Aggie did not; she was able to choose land. Her mother, however, Margaret; needed to return to the sea. The creature that infected me I have no history of, although, I sometimes have a calling to go back. It can find me even out here in these distant oceanic waters. They are maenads.

This Room is a bloody mess. The three carcasses offer enough blood to keep us for a day or two until Sasha is strong, then we can go to the canal and she can purge with seawater. Once her lungs are filled we can go, she can have her dream of escape from this life of human misery.

It was kind of fun to be master over this room. And for the first time in my life…(or whatever this is), experience the freedom of complete freedom. Separate from it all. For example, I can sit here on this heap of corpses, and no one is going to come in or enquire, because the head honcho, the big kahuna, the big ball of wax, manning this whole mess is trampled under my semi part-time gargoyle foot.

Well, one thing for sure, I cannot go on feeling miserable that I am not so human anymore. Oh! And Sasha's eyes- as she becomes healthier, her eyes have taken on the lovely swirl of deep purple and Martian iridescence See, I invented a new color; Martian iridescence, a blend of that Opal heat thing that we all have, as maenads. It is amazing the transformation in her. We are more like ghosts than a vampire. I don't know if Vampire is the correct name for what we are. I mean, we blood lust yes. However, we are not land-based like your typical New Orleans vampire. We are from the sea. I don't even know if I am immortal? I doubt it. The old ones at the caverns might be, but we are not pure. Sasha and I need to get our feet wet now and then or we age quickly… Sasha doesn't like that handicap.

Unfortunately, there is no handbook on any of this. Or if there is, the only living human being that I know of that might have it is John Morris, the Ludi. He might have salvaged it, from the tower, or Olde Fitzy's wunder Krammer. I have to tell Sasha we have to get to him somehow… eventually, one more Atlas Yacht club meeting… brothers do I have a story for you.

The days have passed, and all obligations are met. Sasha and I walk hand in hand along the canal. Sometimes we go to the seashore to recharge our batteries, as we used to say as humans. Other times we take in late-night dinners under the bridges or clumsy fishing boats where undocumented fishermen are always falling overboard. Sasha loves to shop. The money we find on victims pays for much.

She has adjusted quite well to her new lifestyle- resilient girl, absolutely resilient. I made a joke to her over a recent kill. "Honey", I said, we are better than Bonnie and Clyde." Sasha did not know who that was. We are going to take in the movie one day if it ever comes to town.

Passing by a paper stand I picked up a local sheet and read. Still no clues on the savage assault of Gothic girl- last seen alive at Pyre a steampunk hangout, It has been weeks now maybe months, I lost track of time.

Or…Still, no leads on Big shot kingpin, Pieter, and two thugs brutally massacred in red light district…

The bighorn blows all aboard the magic bus; En route to England.

We must be very strong and love each other,
to go on living.

Andre Lorde.

Time passes unnoticed. The simple pleasures that once brought pleasure to our human senses, have less and less impact on our new supernatural existence. The expectation of an autumn day or a summer breeze even the exaltation of the first snowfall, is bringing less excitement as time goes on.

It is plain that we are being exorcised from our human self, removed from the sensitivity and uniqueness of each season. The aesthetic of life is rotting; turning sour on the flesh organism, human spirit diminishing like decaying fruit.

I have observed it in my art as well. Sasha and I leased a fabulous loft space in Belgium so I can now paint, unhampered like I always wanted. We set it up to our ideals. It was a tremendous space. Sasha created a bed and bath in the eastward wing, it was stone and mortar with a fireplace. There were books and objects of curiosity of all sorts befitting a courtesan. It featured Long windows and Edwardian drapes. It was praiseworthy of the princess in her court. All fantasy was at our disposal. However, it was vanity, that we experienced; Intense self-absorption, not the elevation of spirit one might experience when standing before a great work of human achievement, or the excitation of words projected from literature; only naked empty vanity. It was as though the great fireplace Carved out of rock and marble projected no heat.

I had noticed it in myself, I could no longer paint, That is not to say that I cannot duplicate an image, or replicate a still life or landscape, those are mechanical skills. But my attempts in portraiture fall short of any charm. They lack what the Human spirit infuses in them, the warmth of emotion be it joyful or hard-pressed, it is human just the same…that quality of subjective narrative comes from another place, a place that is no longer a part of me, a soul! A soul that depletes a little more with each blood banquet must occupy an infinitely large space, (the soul) It could take lifetimes for it to abandon completely, sustaining a body in small increments as long as the body stays intact to walk the earth.

It was perhaps a year into our transformation, maybe longer, Sasha was standing before a humble window overlooking windmills scattered across the countryside in her homeland of the Netherlands. She asked with an earnest inquiry, a question I dreaded and could not answer.

"Sean, are we immortal?"

"I don't know". He whispered.

After a brief silence, he added.

"I suppose we could be killed, but I don't know if we could die of natural causes."

Sasha looked at him and turned away, reminding him of something human for a moment. A look of concern came over her with a conviction of emotion that was from the old nature, perhaps the last living leaf from a tree that was slowly dying, giving itself up, so it could be born again.

"OH, what will we do with all this time; I mean, look at this." Sasha looked out into the open field and panned across the countryside. Cows were grazing; some farmers were tending to their chores.

"Look Sean, everyone and every living thing have something to do; the birds are flying to their sanctuary…"

Sean was afraid of this. He did not know what the outcome would be, having so much power over life thrust upon another person, without them fully understanding it or expecting it. Sahsa has only ever been tortured and abused her whole life, now she is a gangster queen. Where is the validation, the rationale? There is none in the supernatural world. None in the supernatural world; All merits are removed.

"Hey, what is this chagrin, you seem Tobe getting on." Sean marched her over to a full-length mirror near the hallway and forced her to look. "Look at yourself, you are gorgeous." You are wearing the finest designer clothes from all the best shops from all over the world. We Dine when we want for something we just go and get more. We kill at will and feast on the bounty. We come from nowhere and we belong nowhere, no one can suspect us because we do not exist, we are invisible entities to the real world… the ultimate gangsters.

"What I miss Sean is the status quo, the moving up, the fitting in. We have no status we do not really exist do we?"

"We do to each other; isn't that enough?" He Mansplained, away.

"We no longer play the games, Sean."

Sean held her about the shoulders. He looked into her eyes that were welling up with fire and topaz.

"We are dead Sasha dead to the old world. You have to stop thinking that there is something more out there. That pit of concupiscence that still lingers, it is useless to you now. In time all those old feelings will pass."

Sasha cut in.

"We live off the lives of others. We are not of the living in a sense of love and honor. Is that what you are saying?"

"Yes! -In a sense. We have each other. We have been allowed to witness how temporal living amongst the flesh and blood is, how fragile and calculating they have to be; knowing they have set limits of time. Limited opportunities to make their goals and dreams come true. We can do whatever we want we take what we need and then we move on."

Sasha looks back into the field.

"What they have out there seems nobler. And yet they crave to have what we have, not understanding that living outside of the natural order of things is a blank existence."

Sean touches her face.

"You will overcome those feeling Sasha, you are still struggling with the old life.

Sasha holds him close and sighs.

"Empty".

She retorts.

"Do you regret that I made you like this Sasha? Was I wrong to have saved your life? You were facing premature death and unjust brutality from one of those noble living creatures you are longing for. He was going to snuff out your existence, you had no chance with him, you were doomed from the beginning. You were going to die forever. Did I do wrong? Your father and Pieter were your judge and jury. Pieter was the tallyman who came to collect payment on a debt you were Pawned for. You are innocent now. The debt is paid with blood; theirs, not yours.

It was an act of love Sasha; you don't know how hard it was for me not to kill you myself just for the blood. I held on to that little piece of soul in me that keeps me loving you. I was human enough to know that it was good. The last great remnant of being human was in your flesh not in your blood, in your all too human soul, not your dispensable human heart."

Sasha turned almost bitter to his words.

"Are we innocent now Sean? "We are invisible, as you put it, non-existent in a place where hearts are beating; abiding in a house of magnificent strangers."

THE DUNES FOR LOONS

Doctor Bursar folds up his chair and hands me a letter. I am the new library assistant; If I should accept the offer, to a tiny library section that was installed into the institution, just opened for our exploitation. I am charged with keeping local history, I ask residents their fish tales, research folklore, sort through antique maps. While I have some archival and preservation training, I have no background specifically in maritime history. The pornographic, former librarian and lighthouse custodian decides that I am going about everything all wrong. We fall in love while exploring a historic lighthouse, surrounded by books and cascading documents.

Tuesday;
One of those rare evenings when I manage to take a walk, have hot cocoa, and read while listening to the wind squeak through little separations around the window frames; quiet conversations of people sitting outside the parameters and quiet rooms. After a couple of hectic months of asylum academia, I read to the choir for the third time. The choir as I call them is a group of hopeless catatonics that sit around me as read to them. It is still as beautiful as always and it is always a pleasure to find details I overlooked the prior times, I wasn't so much aware of the other two times. Tonight we are discussing the odyssey. Charlie's modern sequel.

Note to self;
Try new stuff. Put plants in your room even if you aren't the best at caring for them. I have a dead aloe; it looks dead, but maybe not. I am finding plants that are impossible or at least very difficult

to kill and I am trying to neglect them till they die, that is the challenge. I have a window sill of dry skeleton branches belonging to so-called very hardy house plants whose names I cannot recall right now. One was a Bonsai tree; soon it will be a -sayonara tree, slowly drying in the sun. I am attempting to make that dessert recipe in a baking class I signed up for. Even if everything I bake turns out flat- It doesn't matter. Kitty the baking instructor is very nice. She said that in all of us there is a baker that wants you to make chocolate chip cookies. I am only allowed to take the baking class, I am not allowed around the stove for safety reasons. The people in charge of the projects committee are not comfortable with me yet. They think I am high risk. Even despite Doctor Bursars endorsement. He believes I am over the torching stage. That isolated instance of my past was driven by "inner demons". He declared that I am not a Pyromaniac. However, there is a high level of Lunacy that needs to be explored according to him. It would be wise that I was monitored around the kitchen.

If I can seduce Kitty, I might be able to get her to assist me in breaking out o here...

I still listen to new music. I have been meaning to explore some new jazz for a while. The world is full of infinite sources of goodness and the best thing to do is to try and find as many as possible.

Saturday:

Not feeling right about myself. Recuperating from More meds and barbaric treatments. I do not feel safe here. They are scrambling my brain.

My dirty loving antagonist Agatha Fitz Oswald is, of course, at the Library, in the courtyard, at the bell tower; because we both were sent like good children to pick up the laundry for Captain Fitzy. She is wearing a lovely long hound's tooth dress, which I know was on my behalf of me, because, as my fortune teller will tell you, our bell tower celebrates houndstooth. Already the fine people of Constable hook hide under their little hats, and skirts as they prepare for Sunday, they all vote Democrat, I'm sure, The parade will be amazing.

"Ludi, is that what you're thinking?" my arch-nemesis Agatha Fitz Oswald focuses her eyes at your knickers. "is it some kind of...

sock?" It is no secret she and I used to be close before we were married and our "maenads" of honor smartly so, have introduced us to the idea of true vengeance as our vows to keep.

"Did she wear white? I don't remember. Who has the ring? Was it Sean Anthony? No no no…. he is too scatterbrained, here, you take it, John. Who would perform this ceremony anyway? Ah, Fitzy could do it he a ship Captain."

So what is in that box everyone tossing around?

"It is a sweater," not so fast… I want to tell her that when the time comes; when the world gets cold it will go over my body and I will be warm and I will fill my pockets with hot potatoes to keep my hand warm. And I will be able to run around with my demon bride even in the night. "Can you knit me a camel hair shirt; perhaps plaid, or something." I dare not say I'm sure enjoying winter festivities How was your Octoberfest?." *pompous ass. Jack ass, Idiot, buffoon, clown.*

The townsfolk pass judgments on each other, now it has started and they are pleased.

My arch antagonist Agatha, My Valentine, (I know that your lips are sweet, but our lips must not ever meet.)

She thrusts out her hand. a cobalt blue bottle. "magic elixir," she says, "I would expect the whole town knows about your little problem." gossip. "such a shame, my dear." The wind blows around her long dog tooth skirt. - which I *know* she wore on behalf of me - and she struts herself out of the room like royal family. Oh yes, oh yes, she sashays everywhere she goes, beautiful flaxen hair behind her. the bottle in my palm is melting. I will devise how to get her back starting first thing tomorrow. But oh, she is gone. The bell tower is gone. The bell tower echos the message, Rooted in the earth, pointed to the stars away from the sea.

The week, as always, is a long week, for there is much to make and do and bake and read; so much therapy. My Doctor comes home and I mock him for who he is; for he never comes home without checking the state of the loons up and down. He is the kind who loves his work so completely and sets each room like a stage for a great orchestra to come and perform. Wink-a-dink –a –dink- a–dink–a–dink–a–dink–a–doo-- oh what a night for crooning.

I am too ashamed to tell him why so many of the cats and rats and elephants go missing, only to sail the moon cursor tonight and rejoice. His favorite, although not mine, I'm afraid. Plenty of leftovers. Don't look in the cold box boy.

My Agatha "Fitzy"; today, of course, - in a houndstooth dress. Blushing like a bride… an age spot is unartfully covered on her cheekbone, so striking against all of her refinement. Her Father would say it was for her ungraceful nature, and I know mine would agree. I sleep when the medication tells me to sleep, shoving over our best picnic basket tied with a bow. "I made a picnic basket just for you I did, "everything you have done" *all that horrible treasure of old Fitzy* "it seems you're getting rather emaciated." I can't resist one last comment. "I am worried you're about to waste to nothing."

She plucks out its eyes like Saint Lucy and hands them to me… "Yes, if it weren't for you and your old man.," her cynicism the sarcasm is rich "I'm happy now away safe and secure, oh, 5 years." she farts, "So long from now."

"I am counting the days," I tell her, her lips purse. Her lips curse, her lip gloss cross like a finger-Poppin-mama…The fortune teller behind me make a dismayed giggle. Perhaps, by their estimation, I have eaten the dinner completely. I go home to my future wife smiling. She asks where I have been and I tell her, I've been at the Belltower, but your Olde Man he sails anyway because I like to get up to tricks and he doesn't like to disobey Martha. It is a good game we play at night when we are asleep, and dream so completely, I am so in love that I must convince myself to pull the covers over my nose and practice breathing underwater. How silly to wake up for a young girl's moods.

The first week of the full moon: she gives me a maenad tear, lovely glass that shines like her eyes; I need sunglasses to look at it. "I feel so badly for your creatures, and I must remember to practice charity," she says. "it is such a small thing, but do be careful amongst all that thin pine furnishing of your wunder Krammer, which dents so easily."

my Aggie appears at the front door. Just checking, so lovely to be picked up by nightfall.. at night, in a rage, I try it - beneath the table my penis bends easily. I scuff out the scratch with walnut before my Aggie-Fitzy gets back, can you see. I pull the covers off you face do not fear the sea.

The second week: The evil meds, this time hearty with meat. Her dress is a streaked bleeding meadow. My heart each time it sees her collapses on itself. She hands me clothes for Captain Fitzy, since his wunder Krammer continues to go missing, and the charity of his heart is so warm. I am so ashamed I bury all my treasure far by the old tree, where all my treasure is hidden. again, the covers. She is farting again. It, by now, helps me sleep. I have gotten so good at it that I can simply cover my shoulders to feel perfectly dirty and buried.

-Doing quite badly. I go home to him, shaking. Even sick at times he is a good housekeeper,(my orderly), who comes home examining for dust and dinge so I do not fall behind on my chores. Who checks over and being sure I spoke to only him and no one more. Tell me, who else has a man so involved, in this day and age?

The fourth week: a visit from Miss, Camden. Miss Camden is the volunteer outside agitator. She brought Apple pie and goodies. She is dressed in gingham like a Massachusetts whaler's wife. I like a whole heaping of oyster stew with her, for now, her mammas gone, damn it. I say it will return him to spirits, she laughs, a sudden, beautiful sound, even in the quiet of a ghost. Everyone is staring. Maybe it is the dress that is making her quite improper. Maybe it is the farting, I feel the same way. So much is happening and it always seems she knows what is going on in those damn caverns.

She says she heard daddy has left me nothing in the will, which everyone already knows. She says she doubts either of us can live without that chintzy stipend upwards from the hole we're both in. I look at the marks on her they have been at the tower. I tell her to mind her own business, and be careful where she goes.

All quiet on the western front, so final. Her, garishly pretty cloak, she got the sea hag moves, and I in black, to pick up a check that hardly seems the effort. It will be enough to cover my funeral. But nobody ever thinks of dying around here. Funeral. She smiles at me and hands me a cobalt blue bottle. She says quietly: now that I am destitute, there is one thing for it all, and everyone would understand quite completely. It would be quiet, and quick, and complete. My magic is real.

It is the night of the new moon, so dark no man can see in it. I receive notice her Fitzy died, dead, has died, dropped dead, defunct, checked out, and I am sorry to say I find a terrible joy in it. No one should feel joy over another man's death, I wasn't raised that way but then nothing is the same… not today tomorrow.

The air has changed cold. I have left a note asking to be buried in my sweater, the last thing I have made on this earth. I go through each perfect room, but there is nothing else to take with me, for the house has always been moms and Dad's alone, and now aches to be gone of me. I had to trade it into the state for finance in this luxury town run asylum; the Moon cursor would not serve as collateral, HA, HA, …laugh and the world laugh with you cry and you cry alone; would not serve as good tender for it. Having spent so many nights watched carefully, a book of matches and a can of gasoline, I had, would surely set the house ablaze.

I follow her instructions; Quick, quiet, complete.

The horrible rustling is what does it. Like a million interlocking teeth on that houndstooth dress.. and then it is dark, and I am in my coffin, eerie with pine. My head hurts but I must be quick and quiet. They have listened and buried me with my sweater I cover my eyes with it; just go and get it over my head. bring my arms up, dirty shirt, and begin to hit as hard as I can, over and over, the thin wood of the door locked off leading to the wunder Krammer The Magister Ludi gets a crowbar. His favorite furniture is in there- the cretin. It would be oak, of course – The captain left me no money to be buried in any nicer recourse.

the wood splits so horribly, and then it is very hard to breathe, harder than under the covers, and I have to remind myself to be patient and continue to smash at the door, downward and across., while my sphincter clenches and my heart beats so loudly and the whole thing is so heavy it is a universe. The shifting of door hinges is squeaky loud, and echoes and I feel I will be turned into a creature one of them mosquitoes drilling with my beak. And I fear everyone is watching me, or I have gotten the timing wrong, or I will die as a big bug-eyed mosquito, I try to talk but I keep making a humming noise…

But then her hand, and my hand, and we are both touch towards each other, and I am normally not a bug at all. And she lifts me so easily from the deck so tenderly like a plucked turnip and holds me against her, us both panting and wet with misty dew. we can only stay like this for so long, here in that awful Moon cursor, and then we are both running to the old tree where we met, and unburying a second thing; my lovely box of shame, and men's clothes, and all of my worldly belongings beggars treasure Sean Anthony's backpack I have slowly been hiding shit away.

my love and maenad Agatha who has Norwegian blonde hair like a sunset and a mind so fast I sometimes weep in my inadequacy. Who is, even now dirty and raw: even now the only sun in my life!

like this, I am at ghost dawn., and we cleaned by the bay, and her smiling so widely, and only rust on her hands. Her eyes a swirl of ugly garish colors now.. and her delicate breasts and beautiful neck and when I kissed her for the first time it felt like something evil the kind like you always wanted, flowers from an ill-gotten garden; my favorite broken rule, my most pleasurable transgression. Satans money shot., all warm and nervous Grace of sun-burst over a stormy sea, cubbyholes, and cabinet draws filled with every kind of vanity.

I hold her, and she holds me, and we burn, till there is nothing left.

It is one bad dream after another.

The waves crash on the shore on the cliff, sending drops of water into the air. You watch, sitting comfortably in your room at the Dunes for Loons, waiting for the heavy storm to subside. You're sitting, head in hand, and you write in your leather-bound notebook, writing something, anything you can think of. Even though you're declared clinically insane, you're at peace with the world at this moment, this small moment. This limited space.

This dream was gray. Gray is considered by some to be the color of the intellect, knowledge, and wisdom; it is perceived as long-lasting, classic sleek, and refined. It is a color that is reserved and dignified, it carries authority.

Gray is controlled and inconspicuous. It is a color of compromise; perhaps because it sits between the extremes of black and white. Gray is a perfect neutral which is why I can use it as a background for Aggie. It is the story of Aggie. A study in Gray… it is Aggie's story after all, isn't it? The stillness in a relationship, the breathing spaces, the times when you confront your vulnerability.

Slipperyness brings to mind vulnerability.

Lenny came to me in a dream. his eyes were bleeding ink and a pen was sticking out of his balding head.

One bad dream after another.

JOHN MORRIS THE MAGISTER LUDI

The Ludi closed his pamphlet and looked over the works of the exhibition. It was an Ole Worm exhibit that was on tour from the Netherlands. It made its way unhindered from the Plantin Moretus Museum in Antwerp its last European stop, to New York, John morris gazed over the objects of curiosity with a numb curiosity. There were some jars of specimen's embalmed in formaldehyde twisted and demon-like with large bulbous eye sockets with skin pulled over them. How maenad —as he thought. His keen eye passed over maps and crusty books. There were some slim volumes of journals in a glass case; an inscription was inked on to a thin metal engraving." *present my audience with the things themselves to touch with their own hands and to see with their own eyes, so that they may themselves … acquire a more intimate knowledge of them all"* How directly poignant, John thought to himself. Indeed.

The mysterious disappearance of the wunder Krammer that night on the moon cursor haunted the Ludi at least a few minutes every day since it happened all those years ago; the too many near misses, the odd missing pieces. Bronze daggers and Icelandic drinking horns hung about with eerie recollection.

Outside the exit was a kiosk. A Danish man representing the Plantin Moretus printing museum was selling newspapers from around the world. An Amsterdam press release caught The Ludi's attention.

THEHIDEOUSCANALMURDERSANDMUTILATIONS STILL CONTINUE WITH NO CLUE…

Something provoked the Ludi deep to his core. He purchased the papers and some others to find similar instances going as far as London, where gruesome murders were taking place along the Thames.

He thought of Sean Anthony as though by telepathy. Sean was spending time in England from their last correspondence. The connection was surreal, but John had suspected that Sean might have been infected by a maenad that night at the caverns. His suspicious disappearance and the reluctance to discuss why he ran away were making sense now. Slowly putting the pieces together John came to a clue; a slim, farfetched clue, but one only an expert at linking patterns could imagine A key question remained, how could Sean Anthony if he were committing these atrocities to get around town and country so quickly? As a man he could not, but as maenad …

The Ludi hurried back to his apartment, he quickly found the correspondence letters Joh had sent him from England. With some leaves head from the University and some funds he accumulated, he would go to England. The Earls court address was consistent, someone there must know something about him. He began packing and making arrangements.

(Sean Anthony holds the key to the great mystery), thought The Ludi.

(I must get to him somehow.)

Everything was ready, but before he could go, John had to visit his good friend at the library: The scholar Albert Kohn.

John Morris entered the library climbing the stairs that led to the religious studies department. The only door at the end of the hall had a sign that read. Albert Kohn: Jewish and Rabbinical studies.

He knocked softly, a soft voice from the other side welcomed in.

Rabbi Kohn was a pious looking man with a light beard and round spectacles. His office not unlike Johns was a mountain of avalanching books periodicals and papers. His greeting was robust and friendly.

"John, What can I do for you, my friend?"

"I am going away for a while and I need some advice," said John, cutting right to the point.

"We have spoken in the past about the folklore of the Golem. I have taken many notes. I have learned firsthand that folklore is not always the imagination of an ancient tribe or a Brothers Grimm. I will be brief Albert. All you have told me about this creature was not for naught. I have found similarities in it in my own life. And now I am in pursuit of it. My question is, should I endeavor to do this? And can I win?"

Rabbi Kohn leaned back tapping his fingertips together, he straightened up.

"John, you have not told me much. With that being said, I know you well enough to not have to delve too far into your complicated situation. I, as a man and a teacher, knowing what I know; Would advise against it, let it go. That I can tell you; without hearing any more. Everyone has to face their challenges. But I must ask. Why would you want to pursue such a thing, whatever it might be; you are doing so well at the university, you have found peace, why to disturb it over something you cannot win, do you want to go down with it?"

"I was there when it was being created," John said, surrendering, looking unfocused.

"Is it your monster john?"

"Yes, in part."

Have you studied the Kabala teachings we went over, do you understand the formulas?"

"I believe I do, Although I am nowhere near mastering any of it."

"Take your time." The scholar advised him. "The wisdom will reveal itself when you need it." Albert Kohn walked over a wooden shelf and removed a tattered notebook with a plain black cover. He handed it to Sean.

"Take this with you. I hope you should find solace. I think you know what these numbers are."

"I do, thank you, Albert."

Well, then, my knightly friend, you have your answer, you have made up your mind. The dice were cast before you walked through that door. Be careful, and remember what we are, we are human and not very strong, and for the most part, not all that wise. All

Golem, no matter what form they take be it spiritual, physical, or psychological are very old and very wise. Know you limit my friend."

"Thank you, you are a good friend"

The two departed. And John made his way back to the apartment to gather his things and prepare for his flight to Earls court, England the last know place he had known Sean Anthony to take refuge. His funds were limited but he was prepared to take work as a professor anywhere in Europe if need be to complete his quest. Sean Anthony must be found. The secret to eternal life is in his blood.

SASHA

It did not take long. Sasha was becoming very comfortable in her new skin. And Sean Anthony was becoming deeply disturbed. She was becoming more childish and vain; obsessed with her looks. She took on a stylish Goth-like vogue becoming distant and aloof. Her disappearances for days on end were becoming a problem. When Sean Anthony confronted her offering sage advice she would go into a tantrum acting more like a teenage daughter rebelling against a parent than his lover and confidant.

What was more worrisome was the company she was surrounding herself with. She spent nights on end at trendy nightclubs like the PYRE where steampunk and Goth types gathered fantasizing in dark rituals. Sasha was immersed amongst the living with only a blood lust to serve as a constant reminder as to who she was. She was becoming a kind of underground cult princess and playing the perfect part.

I feared that she would become careless in her killings.

For instance; She told me with gleeful defiance how she took part in a bogus initiation cult ritual with some club members, where wrists were slit and she drank freely from the veins of the new inductees. She laughed rather wildly I thought and spoke with cavalier about how she did not have to kill anyone that night. How she got "free blood" from a waiting line of innocent "Suckers". I came home the other evening to find her in bed with two lesbians all three were dressed like it was Halloween in America. Sasha has Scarcely clad in stringy lingerie the other two young girls wore some type of leather steampunk corsets and lace.

"I brought one back for you, "Sasha said withholding an evil grin.

"I thought we could order take-out tonight". Sasha was already immersed in blood feasting from a wound just below her victims the pelvic bone.

The quasi-sexual scene initially repulsed me, leaving me with questionable doubt. I knew Sasha intended to shock, however, the emotion of [hurt] does not exist in my soul anymore, I watched for a little while letting go of this childish assault to me on Sasha's behalf as time passed in a blur, throughout watching the blood flow, I finished off bachelorette number two with a full scourge and lusty attack, ripping at her as though I were raping Sasha; tearing at her and hating her flesh as I had hated Sasha in those intense blood-spattered minutes; afterward, we disposed of the bodies by way of the cinerary garbage disposal in the basement.

It was precisely this unpredictable behavior that was worrying me about Sasha. She was becoming angry and vengeful in her killing; more apparent, however, was her intense, abusive, passive aggression toward me.

I believe she thinks that she was meant to die that night at the hands of Pieter van Griot, that despite all his abuse, she felt a kind kinship toward him. In a twisted neurotic kind of way, she loved him. With that being said, it might not have been Pieter van Griot himself she still felt connected to but the whip and punishment attached to him; The umbilical cord of violence and discipline that for almost all her life had been dominating her; the sins of her father, and now she will paint her pain on me.

She will always have to remain by the canals or somewhere similar, for her need to regenerate by water. That along with a soft sense of extrasensory intuition, I will always be in tune as to her whereabouts or proximity thereof; that is how I will continue to find her; She was fixed in a young girls mind and body when I infected her, neither she nor I have any information as to how these transformations will work out, With that understanding, I know

I have to leave, If I could somehow find the Ludi he might have more knowledge about what I have become. It seems impossible, but still…I feel a quixotic destiny, a gut feeling sharp in its intensity…He is out there. I know he is out there.

A fog rolled in off the canal. Sean Anthony huddled against some pilings. Sulfuric puff balls of light encapsulated the lampposts; the percussion of heels tapping, slight scuttling feet of passerby's behind the misty curtain headed toward a destination could be made out hurrying along the seam of the miasma.

Sean Anthony inhaled the wet vapor. The cool velveteen mist dampened his skin. He removed his clothes under the cover of deep fog, lowering himself into the rejuvenating water. He felt his body transform; elongating, the strength of the sea collected in his arms and legs, his body parts simplifying into a more perfect form. He discovered that the more he willed it the better defined the shape could become.

"I should make it into the channel, I should go to England." He began to swim letting the tide lift him up and over the waves. He headed toward his destiny, feeding on the lite fare of marine life along the way.

"I am Ismael".

THE ASYLUM

Charlie Conliffe lay recuperating in his bed. The confusion subsiding, he just lies there thinking or whatever the scattered thought process is called. These new procedures are terrifying. They are not standard procedure, he is coming to understand. Charlie Conliffe is becoming to think of himself as a transitory patient; a John Doe. Some pertinent questions are flooding his half-conscious mind.

"What are these drug s they are giving him"?

"Why are shocks administered only after clear testimony and revealing facts about the goings-on at Constable Hook?"

"Why are they reading my mail?"

Other things don't add up the way they are treating me.

(For one, I am not insane; any professional investigation into my Psyche by a serious physician could see I am rational, not dangerous. Not psychotic.) So why then are they overloading me with drugs and outlawed procedures such as electric shock? No one is inquiring about me; I am left to rot here until I become a brain dead comatose statistic. There might be others here who have experiences with the caverns… I know there are other patients in my ward that are from Key Harbor…but they cannot speak are brain dead cationic zombies. I have seen things that frighten me more at the hands of these so-called doctors than I have at the caverns.

Aggie spoke of the "outsiders". She called them morgue Rats and mad scientists. Captain Fitzy never left the Moon cursor, never went into town. The townspeople are suspicious of everyone. The eccentric way I was treated at the tavern when I began to ask questions … shuffled off pressured with subtle violence. The people did not seem altogether normal; I had always been around summer visitors and second homeowners. The local flotsam and jetsam are shady. The clandestine lifestyle of the Cropsey whites is more than folk tale and legend, curious people have disappeared in those woods.

I have to get out of here. This is not paranoia; I do not feel safe around these doctors.)

Death does not terrify me— the permanence of it does. If I do not get back to Ludi and Sean Anthony the Atlas Yacht Club might perish along with our discoveries. Ludi and Sean are the only ones that hold witness to my sanity, to the horror. I believe my mail is being censored; any attempt for anyone to contact me from outside these walls is being aborted.

The roller coaster chain of events in my life, up until now is what is keeping me strong. One moment you're alive and full of everything the world offers you, and then for the next twenty years, you're nothing. That is how this place makes me feel, like my life energy, my very soul is being dissected; except they do it on a week to week basis.

Doctor bursar interrogates me, he is not probing my mind for the truth, he simply, and ruthlessly like a Nazi scientist wants to find out what I know about the caverns. When they find out they want, they will most likely collapse my brain and probably kill me. They confiscated most of my books and some of Aggie's journals...The Ludi; he has the bulk of Aggie's journals and many of Captain Fitzy's manuscripts... He might be in danger also. I know they have been censoring mail from him.

Maenads could help me. If I were one now I could shape change into a wolf and rip my way out of here.

Aggie! How I miss Aggie. Charlie went under his bed to search for a satchel where he kept some personal items. He took from it a small suede pouch and emptied the contents into his hand; some pieces of polished glass and shiny seashells piled in his hand. He began a soulful soliloquy as if he were praying.

"The mermaid tears I hold in my hand for you; the polished glass of colors and shapes that washed up on the shore that fated day we met. Did you know that someday I would cry for you, Aggie? Did you ever think that my tears could be as hard as the elegant glass substitutes you shared that morning on the beach with me when you were mild and magnificent and too resilient to shed your real tears?

If only she could come to my window. If only I could hear her gently tapping on the glass; despite that night that put me over the edge, alone in the bell tower, disowned by the world. She sat a sea hag, not a normal girl, not a maenad but a nether girl, a legend to the town folk. Key Harbor had its sea hag; a crazy old crow that stares out over the caverns. The children are scared of her, a true to life legend in the making like A Grimm's fairy tale or a character from Robert Louis Stevenson. I knew her and I knew of her gifts. And if only she were here beside me we could lay this "Dune for loons to waste."

If only her maenad hit squad could swoop in here and clean house, I could be free. He thought to himself.

I cannot die here. I have to get away… I can escape… must escape. If I play the game I can stay alive. No more meds. No more episodes that can get me shocked. I have to get to the Atlas yacht club somehow or let it be known how my comrades in arms can reach out to me. We must meet one more time. All three of us; to each his own, spinning one more yarn beside a hurricane lamp secured in the burnt rubble of the Olde Spye inn.

Meanwhile, the Ludi drapes awkwardly slumped across a bench that is sternly anchored to the floorboards of a rickety ferry. Nothing could be seen here on the English Channel. The night is black like deep space; not a star to twinkle, not a moon. The ocean tonight is more of an ancient mariner than the mariner is of the sea. His hair a twisted nest, his beard a projection of bouillabaisse soup and sprinkled bread crumbs. He has become untidy the last few days letting himself go to a calling that eats at him daily. (They are a third of myself, they are more myself at times than I am, whatever our souls are made of, Charlie, Sean Anthony and mine are the same. I remember that night I watched Sean Anthony painting a seascape pixilated against the harbor lights. It was brisk October, Autumn was settling in. He was abstracting a harvest moon that seemed to be laughing over the bay. I watched the brush strokes dipping into the canvas stirring pigment; correlating, objectifying; trying to solve the riddle of creativity with each stroke, infusing the tar-like water with human interpretation. The black and blue sky with increments of light. He communicated with the moon, making it grin at our lives folly.

In the hollow of its face, it embraces the blessings of weak mortals; They have little but platitudes and poetry to offer. In the conscience of its core, it curses the onlookers, a green-eyed beast in the heart of the sky.